Spitzee Anota

Spitzee Anota

by

D. R. King

LONGMANS, GREEN & CO
TORONTO · NEW YORK · LONDON

LONGMANS, GREEN AND CO
20 CRANFIELD ROAD TORONTO 16

LONGMANS, GREEN AND CO INC
55 FIFTH AVENUE NEW YORK 3

LONGMANS, GREEN AND CO LTD
6 & 7 CLIFFORD STREET LONDON W I

ORIENT LONGMANS PRIVATE LTD
CALCUTTA BOMBAY MADRAS
DELHI HYDERABAD DACCA

FIRST EDITION 1957

PRINTED AND BOUND IN ENGLAND BY
HAZELL WATSON AND VINEY LTD
AYLESBURY AND LONDON

SPITZEE ANOTA

COPYRIGHT 1957 BY D. R. KING

Published simultaneously in the
United States of America by

LONGMANS, GREEN AND CO INC
NEW YORK

Chapter One

TED MACDONNELL rode up the slope to the river bank, along a trail deeply beaten and rutted with wheel tracks. As his little Indian pony jogged steadily along, the lad thought back to the last time he had ridden this trail. Then his mind flashed far back, to the first time he had seen the new country. It seemed so long ago now that he could barely remember the ship that had struck the iceberg, and the whaleboat that had carried his mother away from him, the mother he had not seen again. He could hardly remember her, but bright in his mind was the face of his father, who had taken him from the rescuing ship at York Factory and nursed him back to health. His father had been an important man with the Company then, the Hudson's Bay Company. And in the great fort of York Factory, which was the largest post on Hudson's Bay, Ted had gradually grown strong enough to take an active part in all the wonderful things that went on in the wilderness around.

Now he was returning to Fort Edmonton, where his father might be, and René Corteau, his father's faithful French-Canadian friend. How long ago had it been that they had paddled their way up the mighty Saskatchewan River from York Factory to Edmonton? It must have been all of four years. How things had changed in that time!

He thought of the fur brigades arriving at Fort Edmonton, and he remembered the day he and his father and Corteau had set out for the south country, heading deep into the unknown wilderness where few white men dared travel. He remembered the great decision his father had made when he left the employ of the Company to strike out on his own, the little cabin they had built beside the Spitzee River, the lovely valley of the river, called by the Indians Spitzee Anota, "the country of the river where the trees grow tall". Once again he saw the bright leaping flames as the tiny trading post burned. His father and René had both disappeared then, and for the past few years Ted had thought them dead; but now he knew they were alive, and his heart leaped at the thought that in a little while he might meet them.

But how much had happened since he had last seen them! Three years he had lived in the wild land to the west of Spitzee, deep in the mountains. He pictured in his mind his frantic struggle along the rocky river bottom as he made his way slowly upstream to escape the wrath of the Indians. At first the tribes had been so kind and gentle, especially with his father and René, and then the whiskey traders had come to Spitzee. Ted shuddered at the thought. How he hated them, these rough, unscrupulous men from across the border, outcasts from their own country, seeking refuge and fortunes in this new, wonderful country where the only laws were those of Nature!

Ted could not help thinking of the cruelty and beastliness of these men as they traded their poisonous brews to the natives, laughing to see the helpless Stonies fight each other, and die by the score as they dropped senseless in the brush around the whiskey fort. Then had come the night Ted would never forget, when the Indians had lost control of their senses and attacked even his father's little post, capturing René and his father, burning the post to the ground as Ted watched helplessly from hiding in the woods. When the lad returned to seek shelter at the whiskey post it had been attacked also, and overrun, and Ted managed to escape with only his old long rifle and a little powder and shot. By moving at night and staying hidden during the daytime he had worked his way slowly up the little river until he came out in the deep valleys of the mountains, and there on a hillside he had built his rock-and-mud shelter, dug part way into the hillside for warmth and protection. For three winters he stayed in the valley, finally making his way out to the foothills, where he met his young Stony friend White Calf. The tribes had all been on the warpath against the whites then, but with the passing of two years peace gradually settled over the country, and Ted returned to Spitzee, mounted on a pony, a gift from his Indian friends, carrying his long rifle, as well as a heavy pistol he had found at the whiskey fort. The Stonies had told him that his father and René were safe, and had gone to Edmonton. Now Ted rode up the last hill and looked from the crest down the steep bank to the river. Just across the broad river stood the fort.

9

This was Fort Edmonton in 1871. He gasped as he noted the changes in everything he saw. Houses and barns clustered all around. The fort was packed with people, busily hustling and working, and even as he crossed the water and rode up the trail to the gate, he could hear the sounds of civilization. The gate stood wide open, for there was no Indian trouble this far north. He rode through and into the great yard. For a few minutes he looked around, trying to remember where the main counting rooms were, and when he made up his mind, turned the pony that way. Hardly had he started to ride across the yard before a man called to him.

Ted wondered what all the excitement was about, until he remembered that he had just come from the south country, and everyone in the fort seemed interested to know what was going on out there. They knew there was trouble, but how could a white man ride through Indian territory alone? His own questions about his father and René had to go unasked as he dismounted and began to answer the questions of a growing audience. Finally the last curious stranger moved away, and Ted turned to lead his pony again toward the counting rooms where he thought his father might be employed. One man had stayed behind the others. Now he approached Ted.

"I beg your pardon, young sir," he began, "but I could not help overhearing your story of the south country. I wonder if you might tell me something." Ted looked deeply into the eyes of the older man. "If I am able," he replied quietly.

"I am wondering if you might have run across any trace of a young white lad near the Spitzee River country. He is my son, and I have not seen him for three years."

For a long moment Ted gazed steadily at the other, noting the greying hair, the weathered wrinkles of the face. Then——

"Father—don't you know me?"

James MacDonnell stared at the boy. Was it possible that this brown young man was his long-lost son? Then some inner voice told him it was, and he managed to find his voice:

"Ted? My son? Ted?" and with a cry of gladness he leaped close to Ted, grasping the lad with both hands, laughing a little, even though two shiny tears rolled down his cheeks.

"Three years, Ted! Ted, my son, you're alive! Three whole years." He pounded the boy on the shoulders and back. "We thought never to see you again, lad. We feared you were dead. We heard nothing of you from anyone we met and when no word came before winter, we came back to Edmonton. We left you alone on the prairie!"

"You couldn't have known any different, Father," consoled the boy. "After the Indians burned the post I thought you were dead. I had no place to go except up the river to the mountains."

"But Ted, how did you manage to keep alive? How did you ever get through the winters?" The boy smiled a little grimly. "Oh, I dug a shelter into a hill and made out all right. It was fine once I got used to it, but I certainly learned a lot while I was there."

"I dare say you did, Son." James released his grip on Ted's arm. "But what are we standing here for? Come along, we must go to my cabin."

"Cabin?" Ted asked. "Do you and René rate a cabin of your own in the fort?"

"Why yes." MacDonnell's smile was hidden from the boy but the older man glanced slyly from the side of his eyes. "All married men rate separate houses." Ted stopped where he was.

"Married? Father, what do you mean? Have you forgotten Mother so soon?"

"No, Son," his father chuckled, "but you have. Come along and show her you're still alive."

"Mother! HERE?" Ted's yell made heads turn far across the compound. James nodded silently. Ted stuttered, not quite understanding——

"But-but-but—how—where—when—how did she get to Edmonton?"

"I went to get her two years ago," explained James. "You see, she wasn't lost in the shipwreck as we thought. She was picked up by fishermen and taken to their village on an island. They kept her there for a long time, until she was well enough to travel, and then sent her to Company headquarters at Montreal. The Company knew I was here at Edmonton, so they sent her on to Fort Garry and I got word of it when René and I got back here after we lost you. We went back to get her and brought her out with us. "We feared you were gone, but your mother still dreamed of that little farm somewhere out here. We thought to wait at Edmonton for a few years, until the country was at peace, and we had built up a little more money, then go back to our valley at Spitzee. Now that you have come back to us I know that we can go to Spitzee country and build our home."

Even as he spoke, they rounded a corner and Ted caught sight of the small log house built against the palisade.

James halted and turned to the lad. "It will be better to

let me go in first and prepare her, Son, for she will not be ready for the shock if you simply walk in. I'll come out and tell you when to come." Ted knew this to be sound advice.

"All right, Father, but hurry."

He waited nervously as his father opened the door and went inside. A moment later he came out, and Ted caught the glint of tears on his cheeks as he motioned Ted forward. As the young man stepped to the open door, James spoke to the woman inside:

"Mother, here's your laddie come back safe!" And the door closed behind the boy.

James waited outside until he heard the first glad cry, then he turned suddenly and strode off across the fort yard, looking for his friend and partner, René Corteau.

The French-Canadian was down by the river, and he greeted James with a loud shout. James went to him and in eager words told of Ted's return.

"Leetle Ted? My fren' who is kill by de Injun—he's don' be kill no more?" Corteau could not believe his ears. And even when James took him by the arm and started off toward the house, René muttered, "Dat's pretty wonderful t'ing, I'm t'ink, Jeem. Leetle Ted, de po'r leetle feller—all by heesself on de beeg prairie—all by heesself—de po'r leetle sparrow. By gar, I'm bet hees be scare half to deat', eh Jeem? An' seek too, eh? He's pretty small fellow for be on de beeg prairie all by heesself. *Nom de nom,* I'm be glad for see heem, me. Bet hees be planty glad for see ol' Corteau too, eh? An' bet he be planty glad for see hees momma too."

By this time they were at the cabin door and as they entered, boy and woman looked up at them through tear-filled eyes. The mother and her son sat at a rude wooden table partly covered with a half-prepared meal. Ted looked at Corteau, who stumbled toward him, arms held out in greeting.

"Ted, *mon ami*! Leetle fren'! By gar—by gar!" He stepped back to have a better look. "*Nom de nom*, leetle sparrow, yo' don't look so planty seek. I'm tell you, boy, I'm be pretty scare I'm never see you no more."

As the small Canadian spoke, Ted smiled happily and stood up. He looked fondly down into Corteau's astonished eyes.

"It's mighty nice to be home again, René." He took the little man's weathered hand into his own.

"*Sacré bleu!*" gasped Corteau. "Leetle sparrow—I'm teenk I don' hardly know you—you are so *beeg*!"

"Boys have a habit of growing into men," laughed James. "Come, Mother, let's have our tea to celebrate this great occasion. Our lost boy has been found, or rather, has found us."

By the light of a smoking lamp and the flickering fire they sat long after dark around the table. Ted told them of his escape from the Stonies, of the burning of the fort, and his long trip up the Spitzee River into the mountains. As he told them of his hut and the months he spent in it, he found himself thinking very fondly of that rough shelter in the wilderness. Even though some of his experiences had been dangerous and hard, most of his memories were of the wonderful days spent in the open air, hunting and trapping, exploring and building. And in those three years he had turned from a frightened boy into a self-assured, proud young man. Long into the night they talked, and when daylight came again, James, pride shining in his face, lost little time in putting the boy on public view.

Ted was anxious to return to the Spitzee, but on advice of his father and Corteau, he decided to wait for a while, for things were still very unsettled on the frontier. Then, too, there was much work to be done, much gear and food to be bought before they could start, and all that equipment would take a good deal of money. With three of them working for the Company though, Ted figured it would not take more than the one winter to make their stake.

Even the older men felt the desire to strike out for the South. The first real evidence of such longing came on one calm evening not long after Ted's return. They sat in the dimly lit cabin, Mrs. MacDonnell sewing, the men doing some of the multitude of small tasks that had to be done. Ted and his mother sat together at one side of the room while James and Corteau sorted a small pile of furs they had traded. James thought of the plans he had in mind, seeing his little family happily settled on their own land.

"W'at's dat you say, Jeem?" asked René, looking up from his counting.

"Hm-m-m-m? Oh, I guess I was dreaming out loud, René. I was thinking of the Spitzee country again."

"Ah *oui*, my fren', I'm t'ink you like dat place, eh? I'm hope we go back dere pretty soon."

James bent again over his records, his pen making scratchy sounds in the still room.

"Yes," he said after a few moments, "I think about the valley day and night, now. It's got everything a man would need. There's shelter and game, and logs for building, and grass for stock, and water——" Here he stopped at the look on Corteau's face.

"Water!" growled the Frenchman. "Agh-h-h-h!"

James laughed heartily, remembering Corteau's great

distaste for water in any form. "But think of the soil, René. The good black, deep soil. If it will grow wild grass four feet high without cultivation; why man, man!—think of the grain it'll grow with a bit of turning and proper care. Why, we'll be able to sell some of our crop, and get trade and money for it." He breathed deeply at the thought. "Man, man! It's a gold mine on top of the ground."

From across the room, Ted spoke up. "We'll go back, Father. But we had better lay in a stock of goods and tools, hadn't we? I was offered a job with the post hunters today, and I think I'll take it, for we'll need all the money and trade goods we can get when we head south come spring."

MacDonnell turned to Corteau. "Hear that? That's my son speaking. We're going out together, he and I, and we're going to build the best farm in the whole country of Assiniboia. The best in all of Canada."

"If the country is peaceable next year," Ted cautioned. "You know as well as I that the tribes were mighty hostile when I left them. If the whiskey traders aren't cleaned out pretty soon we'll have quite a time staying put at Spitzee. Let's wait a while and see what the situation is like before we build any more houses."

James winced at this, remembering their first post as it blazed in the wilderness three years before.

"Yes, Ted, I guess I am in a bit of a rush. We'll have to wait till the natives are at peace before we dare take your mother away from the fort. Well—let's get back to work. We've a lot to do before spring, you know."

And the two older men turned back to their tasks. Ted watched for a little while, then went outside, where the streets were filled with the sounds of business. High above the fort waved the blue and gold flag of the Company. The letters H.B.C. stood out plainly and Ted knew they stood for Hudson's Bay Company, but he had heard some of the old hands refer to them as meaning "Here Before Christ." Above the Company flag snapped the red-white-and-blue of the Union Jack.

Ted had been in Canada for six years now, and when he tried to think of his life before that he could hardly remember the trip on the boat that brought him to the shores of this country. The shipwreck was dim in his mind, and he could not recall anything at all about that faraway country of Scotland from which he had come. He belonged to Canada now, and this part of Canada was where he wanted to stay. He took a deep breath, tasting the odours of the fort, the sweet smell of fresh hides, perfumed aromas of harness grease and tanned buckskins. From the open door of the bakeshop drifted the most wonderful smell ever to fill the wild air of this West—baking bread.

Chapter Two

THE rasp of saws in the sawyers' pits turned Ted's eyes that way, and he watched the heavy logs being cut lengthways into long flat boards that would make tables, doors, roofs and floors. The tang of fresh-cut lumber, pine and spruce and fir, wafted across to him, and from the smithy came a sickening smell of scorched hide and burned hooves. Beside the smithy the wheelwright was setting a red-hot iron tire to a yellow-new wheel, making the smoke leap out with a hiss like white water around the bow of a canoe. Ted stood in the middle of the compound, drinking in sights and sounds, and then his eye caught sight of a group of men near the gate. It was the party of hunters making up their pack trains for the coming hunt. Ted walked over to talk to them.

"Howdy, Ted. Made up yore mind yet?" called the chief hunter, Thompson.

"Yes sir! I reckon I'll go along with you this trip," replied Ted. "I'll be ready when you are in the morning."

"Good thing you got yore own hoss," said another man.

"*If* you wanta call that nag a hoss," snorted a black-haired man near Ted. "Where I come from, they'd use that critter fer the baby's rockin' hoss!" A roar of laughter went up from the other men. Ted said nothing. He looked across to the corral where his pony was standing.

"Yep, you shore are lucky," another fellow joined in. "You don't need to worry none about the redskins stealin' that hoss."

Now Ted became interested. "Why should the Indians steal my horse?" he asked. "They'll leave me alone if I leave them alone."

"Not by a darn sight!" swore the black-haired man. "They run off most of our hosses last trip out, an' if I ever get close to 'em I bet I'll get 'em back, an' some scalps too."

"That's right, Son," agreed Thompson. "They near cleaned us out three weeks ago. Got enough mounts for those of us here. That's why we're glad to have you with us. Your horse means a lot on a hunt like this."

"Too bad the kid ain't got a rifle, too."

It was the same man again, calling the insult from across the yard. At his words Ted began to feel angry. He turned to the fellow and shouted: "My rifle is as good as that crow-bar of yours, any day of the week."

A great bellow came from the man, and it took two of his friends to quiet him down, even at the command of the chief.

Then the men gathered around the leader while he explained the plan of the hunt. The band was to divide into two parties, one to be led by himself, the other by Joe Dingman, who turned out to be the black-haired bully. Each

member of the hunting party was to be allotted a wagon
and a driver to carry back his kill, and the men drew straws
to pick their mates. Ted pulled a straw that paired him
with a small crippled man named Jake, and the others bent
pitying glances at the old-timer.

Jake had evidently seen many years of hunting in the
North, but a maddened buffalo had changed his position
from horseback to wagon seat. That he should be part-
nered with a green youth seemed like the height of tough
luck to his older pals, but without blinking Jake simply
took a huge bite from his wad of tobacco and eyed the boy
silently. Once again the bully, Joe Dingman, vented his
sarcasm on the lad. He was shushed by Thompson, and
then they split up, each man to attend to his own preparations for the coming day.

Ted turned back toward the trading house, feeling better
for this talk with men of his own kind, hunters and out-
doorsmen, men who could look after themselves in the
wilderness. He knew that this group of hunters numbered
among them some of the best rifle shots and trackers that
the Company could hire, and he was happy to have been
given the chance to work with them. However, that was
for the morrow, and he must tend to getting his gear in
order. He hurried to the company store to see about his
supplies.

The sun had not yet risen when Ted rolled out of the
warm blankets. He had still not become used to the thick
wool blankets issued by the Company. His squirrel robe,
which had served as bedding in the mountains, was now

rolled tightly and stowed on a high shelf of the cabin. As dawn gradually came, he washed his hands and face in clear, cold water and swallowed a few bites of bread and cold venison, washed down with cups of scalding tea. The good white bread tasted strange after a diet of sourdough for three years. He glanced across the kitchen to the door opening into his parents' room. No sound came from within, so he was relieved that he had not disturbed them. From the room he had recently left came the soft snores of Corteau, and Ted wondered that the woodsman, who once would have been wide awake at the slightest movement, could now sleep through a small war without missing a breath. Civilization certainly spoiled a man for the trail.

Ted silently opened the door and stepped out into the growing light, and from across the square he could hear the low voices of the others as they saddled and packed. The jingle of harness startled him, and he realized that it was a sound which only a white man's horse could make, for the Indian had no metal gear on his trappings. Ted's own hackamore was of rawhide, and he had no saddle save the blankets he laid over his pony's back. The others stared at him as he mounted, and he heard whispers and hidden laughs at his crude riding equipment, but ignored them. He knew that with all their fancy saddles and bridles, not one of these men was a match for the team of an Indian and his horse, especially a horse that was trained to run buffalo.

The company of hunters filed quickly and noisily through the gate, winding in ragged formation along the river trail. Ted rode near the front of the file, watching for signs on all sides. From conversation overheard on the night before, he understood that the method of hunting was to ride to a certain area and drive across the country, slaughtering all game and making quite a holiday of it. Ted did not approve of this idea.

"How far do we go before we hunt?" he asked Jake.

"I dunno!" replied the crippled driver with a shrug. "As fer as the chief says, I guess. Probably camp tonight an' hunt all day tomorrow."

"Any regulation says we can't hunt along the way?"

"Nope, none that I know of. Trouble is, this part of the country is plumb shot out right now. Joe Dingman says they ain't a pound of venison within twenty mile of the fort."

"Well, that may be so," Ted acknowledged, "but just suppose we did happen to get something along here someplace?"

The driver turned to him, sitting sideways as he drove. "In that case, I s'pose we jest load her on the wagon."

"And suppose we fill the wagon while we're going out?"

Jake chuckled before he answered. "Wal now, boy, I reckon we'd jest have to turn around and head back to Edmonton. Mebbe you're thinkin' what I been thinkin' all along. Way these fellers hunt is a caution. Why, the noise they make would scare all the critters plumb to death before we get to 'em. Some of the boys, they like the huntin' trips. Gives 'em somethin' to do, and they all have a mighty good time. Me, now, I'd rather make shorter trips, cause we get paid by the trip, not by the distance we go." He pursed his lips and shot a stream of tobacco juice against a passing tree.

"Maybe we can do something about that." Ted winked slowly. "Will you go along with me?"

The teamster turned to look at the boy again. "I don't

know what you're aimin' to do, Son," he drawled, "but I think you can do it. I'm with you."

"Good man!" smiled Ted. "Now listen, drop back to the end of the wagon line, and when I tell you, pull off the trail into the bush so the others won't see us stop."

"Right!" nodded the driver, and as they rolled on he let the other wagons overtake him. He stopped his team, pretending to adjust the harness, and one by one the others passed, until his wagon was some distance behind the rest. Then Ted rode back to him.

"I told them we'd had trouble and would catch up in a little while," he said. He looked around and turned back to Jake. "Jake, see that next clump of trees we have to go around? Well, pull the wagon in behind it, so you're hidden from the trail."

They moved slowly along the road, now winding between tall evergreens, and gradually the party swung to the left and disappeared. As each wagon turned the bend Jake drew his team more to the side, and when they were the only ones left in sight, he turned in behind the trees and stopped.

"We'll sit here for a few minutes," Ted told him. "Sort of let the dust settle."

"Reckon they's game around here, do you?" grunted Jake.

"Plenty!"

"Figure you can fill the wagon?" Jake would like to see this done, for it was hardly three hours from sunup and he would have time to make another trip if the kid could do it.

"I figure we can get all we want, if you'll sit still for a while."

Ted was using eyes and ears now, as the sounds of the hunters died away in the distance and the noises of the forest came back. For a full fifteen minutes they sat still, not moving, until Jake could bear it no longer. He turned to Ted, and was just in time to see the rifle come up to the boy's shoulder. He looked wildly around to find the target, and managed to spot a slight movement in the brush. His eyes widened as an antlered head appeared, and as he watched, the great body of the elk appeared on the trail.

Before he could make a move, the rifle roared, and he saw the beast stumble and go down. Quick as a cougar, Ted was off his horse, and his knife flashed as he cut the animal's throat. Jake climbed down from the wagon, and together they rolled the carcass a little way off the trail and butchered it, heaving the meat into the wagon. The entrails and feet were buried in a quickly dug hole, so that the smell of blood would not frighten other game.

"Now," said Ted, "will you wait on the wagon until I shoot something else. Then I'll whistle to let you know where I am, and you drive as close as you can and then come into the bush to give me a hand."

Almost before Jake knew it, he was alone. Ted had faded into the underbrush without a sound. There was something unearthly about the way the boy moved.

Jake sat on the high wagon seat and waited. He eyed the carcass, thinking that about four animals this size would be a good load; then his thoughts were interrupted by the sound of a shot. He listened, but the expected whistle did not come for some time. When it did, he drove the wagon close to the sound and left it there. Then he made his way in among the trees, following the whistles that came at frequent intervals. In five minutes he reached the place where Ted was sitting with his back against a tree. Nearby lay the body of another large elk, a cow this time.

"Nearly got away, this one. Ball glanced off a branch, just nicked her. Had to chase her and hamstring her." He pointed to where he had slashed the animal's hind leg to cripple it, before cutting its throat.

This carcass they cut up in quarters to make it easier to carry through the trees, and in two trips had it loaded on the wagon.

Ted looked at the teamster. "Well, we may as well start back now, or we'll be full before we get there."

"Aye, we'll be full twice over if we're not careful," Jake replied with a broad grin. And back they went along the trail they had travelled only an hour before.

At the first creek Ted called a halt. For half an hour they rested in the shade, and this time it was Jake who saw the deer first. Though smaller than the great elk they had already bagged, it was as good to eat. Jake watched Ted raise the rifle slowly, draw back the heavy hammer, and take careful aim. The man looked at the long, light weapon held so rock-steady, comparing it to his own shiny new Ballard. And even as he watched, he was not prepared for the noise of the shot. The deer gave a long leap and dropped.

Jake had the next chance, and he proved himself a marksman when his first bullet brought down the doe. Now they had their full load, and with the wagon wheels creaking under their weight of meat, they rolled slowly back toward Edmonton. When they came in sight of the walls, the lookout hailed them:

"Whatsa matter, Jake? The kid play out on ya?"

"Yeah," called back Jake, trying to disguise his grin

with a frown of disgust. "Didn't get no more'n ten miles out before we had to turn back."

"Tough luck," commented the other. "Next time mebbe you'll draw Joe Dingman and have a real hunt."

Ted pretended not to hear this insult, although the man's voice carried across the compound. The boy winked solemnly at Jake, then kneed his pony into a trot, heading for the Company store. He needed more caps.

Jake kept a straight face and slapped his team with the reins, making them walk a little faster. The wagon passed through the gateway and several idlers turned to watch. Jake drew rein at the long building that housed the great ice pits and meat storehouse. More watchers gathered around to jeer, but when they caught sight of the loaded wagon box they kept silent.

Jake bellowed to the men inside the meat house, and they opened the door to find out who was making the hullabaloo.

"Well, Jake!" cried one. "What you doin' back so soon? Got your load already?"

They laughed loudly at their joke, until Jake replied, "Yep. Give us a hand, will you?"

The laughs died away when he began heaving chunks and sides of meat onto the platform. For several moments nothing was said. Jake could hold back no longer. He looked into their staring faces and burst into hearty guffaws.

"Guess you fellers never seen a real hunter yet. Guess MacDonnell's kid knows his stuff, you bet."

The tongues came untied then. "Great land o' Goshen, Jake, you ain't been gone but half a day yet. Where'd you find all this here game so soon? Joe Dingman, he says they ain't hardly a hare within fifty mile, what with the Injuns campin' close, an' all. Where'd you find it?"

"Didn't have to find it." Jake laughed, thoroughly enjoying his moment of triumph. "We jest waited fer it to find us. Real smart feller, thet young MacDonnell. Now hurry up and bear a hand here. We got another trip to make today, you know. Winter's comin' pretty soon. Let's get a-humpin'." And he swung the haunches and sides faster than the men could haul them inside.

When the wagon was empty, he climbed onto the seat and whipped up the team to a fast walk toward the gate, where Ted was already waiting for him. Together the rider and the teamster went out, while a dozen men watched them in wonder.

"Joe Dingman's gonna feel right sore about this," muttered one. "Mebbe so," said another, "but I doubt if anyone but Joe will worry about it. Least of all the kid there. Seems like he ain't looking fer no trouble, but I bet he kin look out fer himself."

The new partners did not take long to reach their hunting place this time. They stopped on the trail and Ted broke the silence.

"Is all the area around the fort supposed to be shot out?"

"Fer twenty-five miles around," Jake replied. "Joe Dingman claims they ain't a wagon load of meat in ten miles. That's why the whole kit an' caboodle of 'em goes way out to the hills to hunt now. 'Course, there's lots of game for the killin', as you jest showed. But seems lately people are gettin' tired o' real huntin'. They'd rather set in

one place an' let the critters be stampeded past 'em, an'
jest pot 'em off as they come. I dunno—mebbe I'm crazy,
but I bet some o' the fellers I'd make two trips a day with
you shootin', an' it looks like we're goin' to make it."

"Two trips!" Ted grinned at the older man. "Well, I
guess there won't be any trouble doing that. Seems to me
like they waste most of their time in travelling. If we were
to go a short ways out and then do some real hunting, why,
we could make three trips a day, if we're lucky."

"That's the way I figure it too," nodded Jake. "So I
think the best bet is fer us to get off the trail a ways an'
leave the wagon. They's a trail that used to go down to the
river here when we got ice off the islands, but ain't hardly
anyone uses it now. That all right with you?"

"Sounds like a mighty good idea," agreed Ted, and they
started the wagon rolling toward the turn-off. It was not
much of a trail, but they were able to follow it between the
trees, and soon they found themselves in the heart of
the forest, nearly overlooking the river. They tethered the
horses and Jake ran a pole through the spokes of the rear
wheels to keep the wagon from rolling down the slope.
Then they took their guns and set off into the woods.

As they made their way through the trees, a memory
came to Ted of the time when Corteau had first taught him
to use a rifle. That was four years ago, and he had learned
a great deal since then. He put his learning to use now as
the two stalked through the forest, and within minutes they
had sighted and brought down their deer. By taking the
greatest care to move silently, they managed to bag four
more before they decided they had enough. Although these
woods' deer were smaller than the great elk, they knew that
the meat would fill the demand during the long winter

months, and they set out on the return trip with high hearts and proud grins.

"How in tarnation do you fellers git so much game without goin' away from home?" howled the butcher as they heaved the carcasses into the meat house.

"Wal, it's kind of a secret." Jake looked wise and made a show of glancing around to see if anybody was listening. "You see—Ted an' me, we found us a meat mine."

"A *what*?" The man stared at him, eyes wide.

"A meat mine. All we got to do is go out there an' cut us off chunks of meat until we got a wagon load, an then——"

He ducked suddenly as the butcher heaved a slab of venison at him. Howling in glee, Jake jumped on the wagon seat and drove away, his body shaking with laughter. The butcher was left spluttering and heaving as he dragged the meat inside.

Ted had been sitting on his pony a short distance away during the unloading, and he laughed heartily at Jake's joke. When the teamster drove off, Ted followed. He caught up with Jake and the two said good night, for it was later than they had thought, and almost supper time. Somewhere out in the bush, maybe forty miles to the west, the band of hunters and teamsters were setting up camp in a shallow valley, preparing to bed down for the night. The next day they would begin the big hunt. Ted thought of the waste of time and effort needed to drive that far off when game was still to be had within rifle shot of the walls of Edmonton. He rode up to his father's cabin and dismounted, and when his pony had been looked after and turned into the corral with the Company mounts, he entered the cabin to eat his supper with his family.

The next day was a repetition of the first, and Jake and

Ted made two more trips and again returned with full loads. The men of the post were beginning to look at this boy with more respect now, and they no longer poked fun at his old-fashioned muzzle-load rifle. Ted's reputation was beginning to build up rapidly, and even the higher officers of the fort stopped to pass the time of day with James in the trading rooms. On the afternoon of the third day the hunters returned.

For three days of travel, a hundred pounds of provisions consumed and a case of cartridges spent, they had loaded their wagons, all seven, and had even been fortunate enough to bag two stray buffalo that had been surprised in the valley. They were jubilant and noisy as they entered the compound, and when they caught sight of Jake leaning on a hitching rail they hailed him with loud calls and remarks. Jake merely looked at them and smiled, and went on chewing. The line of wagons drew up beside the meat house and they began unloading. The noise and laughter gradually died away, and the waiting people could hear the silence deepening. These hunters were just learning that for their three days of labour they had seven loads of meat among them, while the two lone hunters in two days had come back with four loads. The rest of the wagons unloaded in dead silence, and the party split up as the men turned to their own shelters for the evening meal.

Chapter Three

TED was sitting before the fire busy at melting lead and molding a supply of balls for his old rifle, when there was a knock at the door and his mother went to open it. There stood Jake.

"Young Ted in, Miz MacDonnell?"

"Why, yes—he is." She turned to call Ted, but the boy was already at the door.

"Well, Jake—come on in. What's the matter? Something wrong?"

"Heck no, Ted. Ain't nothin' wrong. You see, it's like this. Some of the boys are goin' out to have a little fun with their rifles. Kind of a shootin' match. An' Joe Dingman— he's goin' to give 'em a demonstration of his shootin'—an' we was wonderin' if—well—mebbe you might jest come along an' watch—an' mebbe—if you have yore old muzzle-load handy, you might show 'em a trick or two, eh?"

31

Ted was highly pleased at this invitation, but he shook his head.

"Shucks, Jake. You know I'm not much heck with a gun. Oh, I know I can hit a deer or elk if I'm lucky, but—well—I've never tried match shooting before. Anyway, I'm sure Joe is a much better shot than me. He's old enough to be my father. He ought to know how to shoot. He's been doing it all his life, I guess."

"Wal, the boys are aimin' to call his bluff talk. They figger to have every man who wants to, try out agin him. It ought to be a right smart show, eh?" Jake winked at the lad. Ted suddenly grew interested. It might be fine sport to see the West's greatest marksmen show their skill.

"Well now, if it's to be a public match, I'd like to see it. When does it start?" The far-off crack of a shot gave him the answer.

"Right now," said Jake, looking across the compound. "Over yonder behind the post, across the field there, by the ravine. Comin'?"

"You bet." Ted grabbed his hat. They strode swiftly across the yard and through the rear gate. Another shot sounded in the still air. They could see a scattering of men gathered around the bank of the coulee that ran down to the river. On the far side a wooden box had been set up, on which was painted a black mark about the size of a man's hand. Ted moved within sight and watched with great interest as the various sharpshooters stepped to the line and took aim. Here was every type of gun imaginable, from the Sharps to the Ballard; Enfields that had seen service in war; new Winchesters that Ted had never heard of before. This was certainly the age of progress, for of all the scores of rifles Ted saw in the hands of the men of Fort

Edmonton, not one was a muzzle-loader. He felt rather glad that he had left his rifle at home, for it would have been out of place in this crowd.

When Ted and Jake first came into the crowd around the match, they were watched by many eyes, greeted by men who wondered silently if the boy would shoot. They found a high point from which they could best see the event, and settled down to watch. One after another the men of the fort took turns at the target. Each man was allowed one shot only, and all those who missed were disqualified. When the round was finished, half of the contestants had been eliminated. Among the second rounders, Ted recognized the famous Joe Dingman and he watched the man closely.

Dingman used one of the shiny Winchester rifles, and its gleaming newness drew gasps from many of the admiring throng. After the second round had been fired, all but an even dozen men were out of the game, and they fell back into the circle of watchers. The twelve men who were left lined up side by side along one wall of the ravine, and the box was replaced by another, with a smaller target, this time no larger than a big coin. In the shooting that followed the number of contestants dropped to five. One by one they dropped out, until only one was left. And that one was Joe Dingman.

"Gee, he's really a good shot, isn't he?" breathed Ted.

"Yep, I reckon he's about the best in these here parts," agreed Jake.

A loud chorus of "Speech, speech!" came from down below, and the victorious Joe was hoisted on several pairs of shoulders and borne to a high rock where he stood above the crowd, directly on a level with Ted and Jake. He held up both hands to quiet the rowdy men.

"Fellas—fellas—I ain't gonna give you no speech. All I wanta say is that I may not be the best shot in the whole world, but by the gods o' war, I'm the best in these parts. An' the best dad-blamed hunter, too, bar none. An' I ain't bein' fooled by no trick shootin' by a smart aleck kid with a smoke pole fer a gun."

As he said this, he looked across the crowd directly at Ted, and went on. "Especially a kid what claims to be a real shot an' then is too skeered to stand up agin other shooters and show us what he kin do."

The crowd turned expectant eyes on Ted now, hoping for some heated reply; but he said nothing and Jake squirmed a little where he stood. When the boy remained silent, Joe went on:

"Now if the younker there would take up a rifle and show us what he kin do, why I reckon we'd know whether or not he's as good as he thinks he is."

At this, Ted could hold back no longer. He spoke in a voice just loud enough to carry across to the other. "If I had a rifle I might not mind giving it a try." The crowd began to cheer, sensing a grudge match coming.

"*If* he had a rifle!" laughed Joe. "I notice you left your old clunk at home. Ashamed to show it with real guns, eh kid?"

Now Ted felt the quick surge of anger flow over him. He clenched his fists and shouted back: "That old rifle may be a clunk, but it can outshoot any gun in this fort, including that fancy doodad you're carrying there."

"Doodad!" Dingman's roar made the crowd cheer again; then they quieted enough for him to say:

34

"Go get yore crowbar, kid. We'll see who's got a rifle!"

But before Ted could move from his position on the rock, he felt a hand grasp him by the arm, and when he turned, Corteau thrust his old rifle and hunting bag into his hands.

"Ol' René, hees t'eenk you got de need for dis mebbee, eh? You do like Corteau hees tell you long tam ago, *oui*! You shoot de pant off dis fellow." And he grasped Ted's hand in his own and shook it confidently.

Ted smiled then, and the crowd howled when he said to them, "Let's go!"

The shooters stood side by side facing the target across the gulley, and they drew straws to see which would shoot first. Dingman won. He stepped to the line and shoved down on a lever beneath the barrel of his rifle, and a shiny brass cartridge jumped into the breach. He took slow and deliberate aim. The gun barked and jumped, but no hole showed in the white of the box. It was nearly dead centre, in the black mark.

Ted had been ready to fire, but now he drew the ball from his rifle and reloaded carefully, tamping the new ball tightly, and priming with fresh powder. He selected a good round cap and placed it on the nipple. Then he drew the hammer to full cock and raised the rifle to his shoulder. The men around him sighed quietly when they saw the gleaming weapon rise. Many of them had faced the wilderness for years with only such a weapon.

Very slowly Ted lined his sights on the black mark on the box. He could see the bullet hole made by Dingman, and he aimed beside it, closer to the centre of the mark. His hand squeezed the stock and trigger easily and the hammer fell. A loud roar went up from the men as they saw the shot, for it had gone true. Now the men were even, and a new mark must be set up.

Joe called for a smaller target, this time no larger than a man's thumb nail. Once again he shot first, and knocked the edge off the mark. Ted reloaded as carefully as the first time and his shot took the bottom off the mark. So far the contest was exactly even. For half an hour the two shot at marks of varying sizes, shapes and distances, but each time they came out so closely tied that no difference could be told between them.

Finally it reached such a point that Ted could stand still no longer. "Well, fellows, I guess you know who's the best shot here now. Any fool can see that Joe's last shot was lots closer to the centre of the mark than mine. Looks like I bit off more than I could chew."

He cradled his long rifle under his arm and started to force his way through the crowd. This had just the opposite effect to what he had desired. Instead of agreeing with him, the older man was suddenly aware that this youth had made a fool of him, and he demanded that Ted stay and meet him in other contests.

"Hold on there, kid. Mebbe you're some shot standin', but I'm wonderin' how you'd show shootin' from hossback."

Now the crowd was happy again, and cheered both competitors. Once more Corteau came up behind Ted. He handed over the rope of Ted's pony, and someone brought up a horse for Dingman.

They went up the hill onto a flat above the river. There a stake was driven at the edge of the cleared land and the course was laid out a hundred yards on either side of it.

The idea was for each man to ride at full gallop past the stake and fire at it, and any mark made on the stick would count. They would take turns until one of them hit the target.

Ted felt a sense of relief flood through him. He was on his own ground now. His pony had been trained to run buffalo, and Ted had been trained to ride her.

Again the older man went first. As he thundered past the stake, he fired from the waist, and the watchers roared approval as dust kicked up five feet behind the stick. It was very close.

Ted trotted to the starting line, checked his charge and priming, and gave his pony her head. The horse seemed to sense the game, for she jumped from a stand into her familiar running stride, moving so smoothly that she seemed hardly to touch the ground. Ted raised the rifle to his shoulder, and as he flashed past, sent the ball through the edge of the stake.

The crowd was silent now, for the men knew they were seeing the show of a lifetime. Once again Dingman tried and his bullet knocked twigs from the nearest pine. Ted drew back to the line again, and on the second run sent the ball close enough to just nick the post. A third time Dingman fired from the waist and a third time he missed altogether.

At this, Ted did something that he had never done in his life—he began to show off. After all, he was still only a youngster, and a crowd's applause has turned older heads than his. Charging from the starting line, he blasted another hole in the stake; then, without stopping or reining in, he wheeled his pony around at the end of the run, riding out in a circle around the crowd. And as they turned to watch him, they realized that he was reloading on the run, pouring powder, ramming shot, priming and capping, all from the heaving back of a racing mount.

His circle ended as he finished loading, and without pause he once more went thundering down upon the mark, and again scored a hit. Time after time he did this, until the post, cut in two by the rifle balls, toppled to the ground. With a wild whoop Ted circled around the crowd again, and raising the long rifle in the air, fired a victory salute over their heads. Wheeling sharply, he drew his horse to a halt close by Corteau and Jake, and jumped to the ground, panting a little and laughing.

"By gar, leetle sparrow—ol' Corteau hees not teach yo' dat!" exclaimed René. Jake croaked something incoherent and limped away to brag to his cronies about 'his' hunter. The crowd surged around Ted and René, and amid the poundings and handshakings Ted did not notice the figure of Joe Dingman as he pushed his way through the mob.

"Son," he said, "I'm mighty proud to know you." The circle widened around the two and the men fell silent to hear what their old hero had to say to Ted.

"You're a mighty fine shot, young MacDonnell, and a mighty fine rider. An' you got a real hoss there. An' as fer yore gun, why I reckon it's as good as any ever made by man. Only one thing makes me wonder about it. Now, these new guns here, they hold six shells——" Ted knew the question that was sure to come; he quietly slid his hand inside his hunting pouch.

"But this here weapon of yours," Dingman went on, "it can't shoot only once an' then you got to reload. Suppose, now, jest suppose them there crows there was red-skins. Suppose they was after yore scalp. All right, so you get off one shot at 'em, but the other two, they keep comin'. What are you gonna do?"

"*This!*" said Ted, whipping his hand from his pouch. He blasted three shots in quick succession at the crows that were flapping lazily overhead. One of them dropped as the explosions roared across the plain, and the crowd flinched from the blazing thunder of the forty-four.

Chapter Four

THE winter gradually passed. Ted made many trips with Jake during the days which followed. And he took part in more shooting matches, until his reputation spread up and down the river. Almost before he knew it, he was nineteen years old.

As soon as the snow disappeared from the prairie, the boy began to feel the old urge to travel. He grew restless as he waited, putting in his time doing odd jobs around the fort. His father noticed, and one day spoke to him about it.

"Ted, I know what's wrong. You want to be on the trail south again, don't you?"

"Yes, Father. Somehow I want to see Spitzee country again. Can't you give up your job here and come with me? René wants to get away, I know, and the three of us could ride there in a week, stay for a month or two and build the cabin and barns, and then come back here for the winter.

Can't you come?" Ted pleaded. But he knew the answer before he asked.

"No lad, I'm still employed by the Company until summer. When my time's up I'll be free to ride with you, but I'm not going to try to stop you now. Ride to Spitzee if you like. I'm sure you'll be safe now, and I'm sure you'll know how to look after yourself after three years there alone. I'm afraid that René can't go with you either—but go ahead, my boy. We'll come when we can. I don't suppose the Indians will bother you, will they?"

"Oh, the Indians are friendly enough, but I do wish you could come. Anyway, I'll ride south alone and look over the country. Then I'll come back and help you and René pack our supplies back to the valley. Will that be all right with you?"

"Fine, Son. We'll be waiting for you later in the spring, then. You've given your notice to Mr. Thompson, have you?"

Ted suddenly remembered that he had been working for the Company too; but hunters were employed only when needed, and now that the summer was at hand many of the men who wintered at the fort would be going out on their own for the summer months. Ted left his father then, and went to find the chief of hunters.

When he climbed onto his pony three days later, his father and René were there to say goodbye.

"Take care of yourself, Son," warned James.

"I will, Father. And if I don't come back in a few weeks, don't worry about me. I want to see what the valley is like at Spitzee, and if I can I'll find White Calf again. Of course, if I run into bad weather or if I stay longer than I should and winter sets in early, I may stay with White Calf until I can get a chance to get back here. I've said goodbye to Mother. Tell her I'll be all right, and don't let her worry about me. I'll be safe when I find White Calf and his band." And with a carefree wave of his hand Ted turned the pony and headed out of the main gate, crossed the river and rode up the trail to the south bank.

The weather was warm, although the ground was still frozen hard enough to make the horse's hooves ring on it. Ted turned eagerly into the now well-worn trail, feeling the solid bounce of his hunting pouch against his thigh and the hard lump of his rifle beneath his leg. Once again he was on the prairie, alone and unafraid. He rode happily along, following the twin tracks of the new wagon trail. He was headed back to Spitzee Anota.

Ted pulled his pony to a halt at the crest of the long hill. He sat quietly for a few moments while the horse cropped a tuft of prairie grass. Though he was only nineteen, he had already had years of experience in the wilderness, and he felt no fear or uncertainty as he looked across the empty miles.

He thought of his friend, White Calf, the Stony boy who was his adopted brother. He had not seen him for the whole winter, but surely it would not be difficult to ride to the Spitzee crossing and locate the band of White Calf's family.

The snow was nearly gone from even the deepest ditches, and Ted knew that a few more days of this spring weather would see the end of the drifts. He shifted his old hunting pouch across to the other side and felt behind him to make sure that the bag of flour was securely lashed in place. His winters in the mountains had shown him how important a little flour could be out on the plains. Meat alone was hardly enough to provide the food he would need to keep strong and healthy.

He had been travelling since sunup, and when he looked up at the sky the sun stood high overhead. In half a day he had covered many miles, and right then he was in the very heart of Indian country, in Blackfoot territory. He would have to ride through it for many miles yet, nearly three days more, until he came to the valley of the Spitzee River. So far he had made this trip four times, and had not yet seen Blackfoot sign in all this territory. But their war with the Crees was still very much alive, and the lone white man could never be sure that he might not walk into the middle of a fight.

Thinking of the trouble that might lie ahead of him, Ted felt inside his pouch and took out a small bundle wrapped in white deerskin. He unrolled it and held up the necklace of grizzly-bear claws that he had won in the mountains two years before. He thought of the great bear as he ducked his head and slipped the necklace around his neck. How proud he had been to wear the claws, and how excited his Indian friends had been when they saw the decoration! They had told him that the man who wore such a necklace was considered a great hunter, for only a very few could boast of having killed the 'devil bear'.

The claws were polished and worn now, for he had kept them clean and shining, and he tucked them down inside his shirt. For some reason he felt better with the necklace on, although he knew that his white friends thought nothing of it. But he hoped that the natives of all the tribes in these territories would honour it as the Stonies did.

Now the pony lifted its head, and Ted knew that the time had come to be going. He nudged the horse with his heels, and they started down the hill, moving steadily. Ted sighted a rise of land on the horizon and kept his direction toward it. The prairies were still damp from the winter snow, and all the brown grass lay flat on the ground. In a week or two it would dry and slowly lift until it stood upright again; and when the new green grass grew in, it would cover the whole land like a deep carpet.

Ted began to feel a little hungry. He had eaten nothing since early that morning. The trail sloped a little, and when he came to a tiny stream, he decided to have a bite of dinner. He drew rein at the water and climbed from the horse's back. The animal deserved a rest, so Ted untied the blankets and flour, allowing the pony to drink and graze. Ted knew the horse would not stray, so he let it go where it wished. He started to open his pouch, but first a drink would wash the dust from his throat. He lay flat on the ground and leaned far over the water.

Before he could take a sip, his pony whinnied. Now Ted had spent several months in the busy fort of Edmonton, where horses outnumbered the people, and he took no notice of the sound. It was not until he had sucked up a cool mouthful of water that the thought of danger struck him. A horse will not whinny unless there is another horse near by.

In one long leap he reached his gear where it lay piled on the creek bank. He grabbed at his rifle and ripped it from the sheath. Another great leap carried him behind a low clump of buckbrush on the sloping hillside. He lay flat behind it, rifle up and thumb on the hammer, ready to cock it if necessary. The pony whinnied again, and Ted watched it. The animal's head swivelled toward the direction of the oncoming horse, and Ted faced that way, watching.

He turned his head and laid his cheek against the grass, so that his ear touched the ground beneath. Very faintly he heard the hoof-beats. They were some distance off, but coming steadily toward him. He could not tell whether the horse was ridden, or whether by a white man or Indian, but a few minutes would show him. Ted lay quietly, watching his own horse, and keeping one eye on the trail. Then he began to pick up the beat of hooves without listening for them, and in another minute the horse came over the brow of the hill.

At first glance Ted could see that the rider was a white man. But the man was not a very wise traveller, for all the while he rode, he kept his eyes to the trail. And this was strange, for across his thighs he carried his rifle, as was the fashion of most hunters. This was so that the weapon would be ready for instant action; but this fellow could not be much of a hunter, for he would never see much game if he kept his eyes on one track.

The newcomer approached a hundred feet before his horse caught wind of Ted's pony, and began to nicker and prance a little. The man's head snapped up then, and he caught sight of Ted's pony. The rifle leaped to his arms and he looked wildly around for sign of enemy. But before he could see or do anything, Ted called to him:

"Stand still right there! Keep that rifle pointed down."

The man froze in his saddle, knowing that somewhere a weapon was pointed at him.

"Who are you?" Ted asked him, not showing himself. "What's your business in these parts?"

"I'm white, stranger. And I'm not lookin' fer trouble," called out the other, finally spotting Ted's position. "If it's my money you're after, you're out of luck. All I got is

45

what I'm wearin' and packing in these here bags." He slapped the leather saddlebags on either side of him.

"I'm not after your money, mister," Ted laughed. "I just don't want to take any chances. I've met a few bad characters out here."

"Well, you don't have to worry none about me, friend. I'm out to do a little wolf hunting down south. Aim to meet up with a couple of buddies somewhere along the line. That's why I ain't got nothing with me but what I need fer the trip. But say; listen here——" his voice became indignant. He shifted his rifle and sat up straight in the saddle. "Who the Sam Hill are you, an' what right you got stickin' up peaceable traders? You own this here country, or something?"

"No, don't own it, but I aim to stay alive in it," replied Ted, standing up and cradling his rifle under one arm. "My name's Ted MacDonnell, and I'm goin' down south, looking for homestead land."

"Homestead land!" snorted the other as Ted walked up to him. "You gonna build a home in the middle of Blackfoot country? You might as well build on a cloud, 'cause that's where you'll end anyways, playin' a harp."

"Oh, I think the Indians will settle down pretty soon. Anyway, I'm headed for the Spitzee River country, and it's only Stonies there and I'm friendly with them."

"That so?" The man thought for a moment. "Reckon two of us would be safer travelling than one. How's about riding along with me, keep each other company, sort of?"

"Sounds all right to me. We've got three days yet to go, I'd be happy to have company."

"My name's Kindell, George Kindell." He slid from his saddle and let the horse drink. Ted put his rifle away and waited, wondering what kind of wolf hunter this man would turn out to be.

"Wolf hunting, did you say?" asked the lad.

"Yeah, seems like the easterners want wolf skins now, 'stead of buffalo. Make hats or something out of 'em. All I know, a wolf pelt'll bring more'n a beaver now. I aim to get me a pile before they lose all their winter hair. Ought to make a bit of money at it, I think."

They mounted then, and Ted led the way along the trail until they topped the next ridge, where he looked carefully across the land before allowing the other to ride up. Then they rode side by side for the rest of the day. At dusk they rolled in their blankets beside another stream, and were up again before daylight, moving before any possible enemy would be alert enough to notice them. After the second night they reached a large river, and here Kindell decided to wait for his friends.

"Ought to be along any time now," he declared. "I reckon I'll just set up shop till they get here. Might make a few pelts while I'm waitin'. Besides, they got the wagon and team. I'm just supplyin' the dope."

"Dope?" asked Ted, frowning.

"Sure—you know, poison." He drew a small glass bottle from one saddlebag and showed Ted the large red skull and crossbones on the label. "Arsenic," he explained.

"But—what's it for?" Ted still could not quite understand.

"Ain't you never poisoned wolves before?" asked the man, amazed.

"Why no—I never killed a wolf any way before. What has poison got to do with it?"

"Shucks, easiest way o' huntin' you ever saw. Way we do

47

it, we go out on the prairie and find a buffalo. Then we run
it down and cut it open, and real quick-like pour in some
of this dope. Got to get it in fast, before the critter dies,
though, so the bloodstream'll carry it all through the meat.
Then we jest leaves carcass where it lays, an' mark it so we
know where to come back to. Day or so later we come
along, and like as not they's mebbe four, five wolves layin'
dead close around it. Wolves don't usually eat dead meat,
but if they're hungry an' the kill's fresh they'll take it.
Beats shootin' all hollow."

"Yes, I guess it does," said Ted weakly. In his own mind
he wondered about what happened to any of the other
animals that might get hold of the meat, hoping no Indian
dogs would take the bait. He knew that when an Indian's
dog dies the family often would use it for food, and what
would kill a dog would certainly kill a man. He shuddered,
but said nothing more. With a wave of his hand he took his
leave of the wolfer, somewhat relieved to be alone again.
And alone he travelled all that day, until he came to the
valley of Spitzee.

The valley was deserted. Not a tepee, not a campfire
could he find, though he rode up and down the banks on
either side of the crossing. When he found no trace of his
friends the Stonies, he headed upstream toward the place
where his father, Corteau and he had built their tiny post
years before.

The clearing was hardly recognizable now, so overgrown
had it become. Ted climbed down from his pony and tied
the animal to a stump. He wandered around the charred
ruins, kicking and poking, thinking back to that night when
he had seen the cabin in flames, the roof falling in in a foun-
tain of sparks. Everything was different now. The stumps

48

of the trees they had cut were mouldy and some were hidden in new growth. On all sides of the clearing the bushes and grass had advanced so that the opening had become almost half the size it had been when they had first cleared it and the long lines of silent natives had wound through the trees.

The same old, weathered trees still stood, Ted noticed, and again he remembered the day he had found the skull. How many more bones were there on platforms in the trees now? And he thought of the whiskey post upstream, by the Medicine Trees. Almost before he was aware of it, he was on his pony and headed west through the bushes. The trail was still clear, so Indians must have been using it regularly, he thought. At the crossing he reined in to sit and look for a moment. The Trees stood just as they always had, their great trunks almost touching, seeming no different from when he had last seen them.

The branches of the trees around were still bare, and through them Ted could see the whiskey post, still standing. It appeared to be deserted also, for no sound or smoke rose from it. He forded the stream and approached the wall. The sun was high in the sky, and had there been any traders in the fort, they would have been up and working long ago; so Ted felt no fear as he rode straight to the gate.

The gate had not been opened for some time, judging from the way it sagged against the ground when he pushed against it. But there was not much need for a gate anyway, for the walls of the enclosure were blackened ruins in some places, where the Indians had piled brush against them and set them afire. Fortunately for the men inside, the logs had been green and had not burned well. Most of the buildings were still in fairly good condition. Ted found a hole in the palisade and climbed through.

It was almost like living in the past, to see the rough cabins with doors gaping and roofs sagging with decay. Grass and flowers grew in a tangled mass from the sod roofs, almost hiding the rotted timbers. For two years he had not seen this post, save for a quick look as he rode past on his way to Spitzee from the mountains. It was the second time the post had been burned, and he guessed that now the whiskey traders had given up. They had moved out and set up posts in other parts of the country.

Ted sat on a crumbling bench in one room and thought back to the things that had happened so quickly in such a short time. Only four years ago there had been nothing here but grass. Then had come the whiskey peddlers, bringing their reign of savagery and murder. Under their hands the valley soon rang with sounds of violence, and death became a commonplace.

This post by the Medicine Trees had been only one in a string of outposts, and being the central fort had housed the rough band of men who called themselves the "Spitzee Police". From this point they were called out to defend other posts that might need help. Part of their job was to discourage those who wanted only to help the natives by trading in guns and powder and other things that would be useful to them. In time the whiskey posts stood triumphant throughout the whole of the prairies.

Now the Indians had finally brought their own justice to the evil whites, and Ted was glad that things were beginning to quiet down in his valley. He thought of the men, Jukes and Taggert, and of Ford, who, Ted now realized, must be some kind of deserter from the American Cavalry, for he always wore the blue trousers with the yellow stripe. Indeed, now that he thought of it, he was sure that these men from across the border were all desperadoes, probably driven out of their own country and forced to band together in order to stay alive in this strange, wild land of Assiniboia, where their own law could not reach, and where there was no law save that of the men who lived there.

Finally, Ted tired of thoughts about the past, and he rose and went out of the compound, not looking back or thinking more of the events that had taken place there. He mounted and rode back down the river. He was determined to locate the Indians and find out definitely whether they were friendly and the land safe for homesteading.

Chapter Five

As he rode, Ted searched each side of the trail for any sign of Indians, but he could not see the slightest trace of fresh hoof or moccasin prints. The country seemed deserted. Wherever he looked, the only living things were the saucy brown gophers that chased each other across the grasslands from earth hill to earth hill.

Ted's pace was leisurely, for time meant nothing in the spring. He camped each night by some small stream, and killed what game he needed for his meals. And as he progressed he became more and more uneasy. Not a sign of Indians had he seen in two days of travel. On the third day he had almost reached the junction of the two rivers where the whiskey post of Whoop Up was located.

Certainly there was something very mysterious here. He rode more slowly, holding the pony down to a walk. His straining eyes finally picked out something on a low rise to the east, and he turned toward it. As he rode closer he saw what he had been hoping he would not see. There could be no mistaking the circle of stones, and Ted felt himself turn cold inside when he saw the little pile of bones inside the ring. He knew the bones were those of an Indian, most likely Blackfoot, for it was their custom on the plains to lay their dead on a hilltop close to the sky where wind and weather soon carried away the gifts and possessions, while crow and magpie and coyote quickly stripped the body of flesh and scattered the bones about the circle.

Ted gazed down upon the remains, and when he raised his head he could see, on nearby heights, at least twenty such burial places, some marked by rings, some by cairns, others with even part of a burial tepee still standing, for sometimes great men of the band were laid in their own tents and left. Some deadly power had destroyed these people, some new and terrible power, and Ted had an idea what it might have been. He travelled farther toward the south, and with every passing hill he counted more graves, until soon the country was dotted with rock piles, like giant gopher hills.

The first sight of the fort also brought him the first sight of unburied skeletons, and from the edge of the river bank he could see many more lying scattered about under the nearby trees, all white and shining in the sunlight. The bones had been cleaned by scavengers and polished by wind and rain.

He knew that in this place there was no plague or war that wiped out whole tribes, but only the curse of white man's whiskey. When the natives traded their finest furs or horses for cups of the horrible stuff, they became like wild beasts, demanding more and more, and would sell their own children into slavery if possible. Those who had the goods to trade for more than two or three cups, soon became blind drunk, and in their madness they often staggered across the prairie, to fall and freeze to death if the weather was cold, or to plunge into frenzied argument with old friends, often with the result that small battles broke out and were not stopped until many Indians lay dead. The younger braves, not satisfied with having their spree among their own, became so maddened that they staged raids upon the fort, demanding more whiskey, and receiving instead death at the muzzles of the fort rifles.

When Ted rode down upon the post that day, he saw that the ground around it was bare and trampled hard. Even so early in the season trade had begun, though there were no natives in sight as he approached. He rode straight for the gate, and before he could give a shout, he was met with a harsh challenge:

"Lookin' fer trouble, stranger?"

"No," he called back. "Looking for a free meal!"

"Wal, thet's what I calls straight talkin', stranger. Reckon we can do somethin' about that."

The man on the wall called down from his perch to someone inside, and in a moment Ted heard the scrape of timbers and the great gate swung open a crack.

"Ride on in, stranger. We're only fightin' Injuns. Got a right good cook here."

The man who held the gate open motioned with a move of his head, and Ted kicked his pony into a trot and rode through. As soon as he was inside, the gate was closed and a huge timber fell across to bar it. Then he dismounted, and a group of men came out of a cabin close by.

"Welcome to Whoop Up, mister. Aker is my name, but

54

my friends call me Dave. These boys here is always glad to see new faces, if they're white. Been kinda quiet lately."

"That so?" asked Ted politely. He would have liked to say something about its not being strange, since there was nobody left in the country to cause any excitement. However, he left his thoughts unsaid. It might happen that he would need the help of these people before the winter came, and he did not want to make enemies of them. They looked like decent young men, on first glance, but Ted had only to think of the bones outside the fort to realize what kind of men they really were.

"Don't tell me these are all the men you have here?" he frowned. "I heard at Edmonton that you had fifty or more and that the country was full of hostile Indians."

"Full of dead ones now," laughed one of the men, and another nodded wisely.

"Only good Injun is a dead one!"

Ted had heard that expression before, from the traders at the Medicine Trees. He was again tempted to make a remark, but held his tongue.

"Where's this great cook I hear you brag about?" he asked. "I'm so hungry you can just cut the horns and hooves off a buffalo and I'll eat the rest raw."

"Don't need to do that, stranger. Supper's about ready anyhow. Come on!" And the man Aker led the rest into the largest of the buildings in the compound. The wonderful odours of roasting meat filled the room and the men sat down along rough tables where great platters of food waited for them.

"Just in time, I guess," smiled Ted. "Lucky I got here when I did, to get an even start."

"You been a minute later, there wouldn't of been nothin'

55

left but the bones," grunted a bearded youth across the table.

Ted helped himself to meat and bread and fell to eating with the others. When the meal was finished the men sat around in the glow of the fire, some smoking, some working on weapons or repairing clothing. As they sat, they talked of many things, but mostly they discussed the Indians.

"Got to drum up some more business pretty soon," complained one. "We ain't taken in enough this week to pay fer the likker."

"Yeah," growled another. "Seems like we're runnin' out o' customers."

"Mebbe we better set up some more posts farther out on the prairie."

"Don't you use the fort at Spitzee any more?" asked Ted, knowing the answer, but pretending innocence.

"Too much trouble out there now," growled Aker. "Too dangerous fer what we get out of it. We built that post twice now, and they burned us out both times. Pretty good spot, though. Mebbe we'll go back there one of these days."

Ted felt chills run up and down his spine when he heard these words. To think of the whiskey traders coming back to the valley! He sat in silence, listening to the talk of the others. Then he suddenly remembered that his first question had not been answered. He asked it again.

"Where's the rest of your outfit?"

"Oh, they've gone out on a little party," said Aker, and at his words the men burst into laughter.

"Some party!" crowed one. "Sure wisht I could of gone."

"What kind of party do you mean?" Ted sensed something evil behind this talk. "Are they out hunting, or some-thing?"

"Out hunting *for* something, is more like it. An' they'll get 'em too."

"Hope they wipe 'em off the map!" cried a grey-bearded fellow.

"Hope they give 'em what they tried to give us!" shouted one from the corner. Now the whole group was talking at once. Ted could hardly make sense from the noise.

"What are you fellows talking about?" he yelled above the din. The loud talk died away, and Aker explained:

"Bunch of redskins jumped us last week. Near killed a couple of the boys, too. The fellers are goin' to teach 'em a lesson. We set out a couple of kegs of whiskey fer 'em, 'nuff to float an island; an' the boys is goin' to trail 'em to their camp, an' when they've drunk all the likker, an' can't stand up, why the boys will give 'em what fer. Ought to be easy as shootin' fish in a barrel, eh?"

Ted felt his stomach turn at the thought of the murder. So these were 'civilized' white men! He wanted to jump on his horse right then and ride to the aid of the defenceless Indians, but he calmed himself, for he knew that if these men thought he might spoil their fun, they would murder him too. And besides, he did not know where the Indians had gone, or even what tribe they were.

While the other men left the cabin to go to their own quarters, Ted sat in the cook shack with Aker, talking of other things. It was very dark outside by this time, and he could hardly set out across country now, even to get away from this evil place. He accepted Aker's offer of a bunk for the night and followed the man to a small log hut. His pony had been taken to the corral and was being looked after, so he went to get his blankets. That night he slept on a hard wooden bed again, and his sleep was filled with visions of dead Indians.

Next morning while Ted wandered around inside the fort, he noticed that something seemed queer, but for a while he could not figure it out. Then quite suddenly he knew what was wrong. The fort, which seemed very large from the outside, was much smaller inside. When he inspected the walls he was amazed to find that there were actually two walls, built about ten or twelve feet apart, of solid, squared logs, and braced by cross walls that divided the space into compartments. These divisions formed most of the living quarters and shops.

Each corner was built higher and stronger than the walls, forming blockhouses that gave the defenders full command of the country all around the fort. Long narrow slits along the wall reminded Ted of the loopholes from which the men at Spitzee had fended off their attackers. Clearly, the walls could withstand everything the natives might hurl at them, but the one weak spot seemed to be the gate. Ted strolled over to look. He was more than surprised to find that it was built of solid oak timbers, nearly a foot thick, with only the tiny trading window cut into it, and this window was just large enough to permit the passage of bundles of furs and containers of whiskey. The gate was closed by a giant bar.

Ted could not help wondering where the oak had come from, for it was certainly not native to the plains or mountains. They must have hauled it in by wagon from farther east. One of the men was stationed on the wall as usual, and Ted called up to ask him about it, but he did not know. He did tell Ted, though, that even the chimneys had iron bars across the tops to keep Indians from entering that way. This fort was considered the strongest on the plains.

Ted watched a few dirty, sad Indians come to the gate to trade, and he could hardly keep from crying out to them when he saw them hand in bundles of hides or pieces of their beautiful clothing in return for the cupful of vile whiskey. He wanted to tell them to take their possessions and run far away from this white man's curse, to throw the evil drink in the traders' faces and go back to their own families. But he could not do so, for even though the traders might not kill him for it, the Indians would not listen. Still, his heart cried out to the natives. He could stay in this place no longer. But even as he turned to go to the stable for his horse, the signal of alarm sounded through the compound. Every man in the fort took up his rifle and grabbed ammunition. Each man had his post and stationed himself where he had been ordered. Ted held his rifle and waited.

There was no need for alarm, though. The cloud of dust that told of the coming of a large number of riders revealed the returning war party from the fort. Ted held himself in control as the gates swung open to admit the returning riders, and the walls shook with the noise of greeting. Shots were fired and shouts and curses filled the air.

When the din and dust settled, and the men were seated in the cook shack, they told their story.

"Nawthin' to it," guffawed one, the leader. "We tailed 'em right up to the hills out east, an' found their camp. They was camped on a river bank, only the river was nearly dry, so we jest snuck up the bed neat as you please. They didn't have no guard or nawthin'. They was all too busy drinkin' to worry about watchin' fer trouble.

"The bank of the river was about this high"—he put his hand to his chest to show them—"an' made a dandy trench. We watched 'em an' jest waited till they was all so drunk they couldn't stand up. Then we let 'em have it." Whoops of joy and yelps of triumph rang through the room. "We jest stood there an' near massacred the whole bunch. Only a dozen got away, I guess. Man, we mowed 'em down, bucks, squaws, papooses, everybody."

He stopped talking long enough to tear off a great mouthful of meat, before he went on with the grisly details. He was deep in the story when Ted walked out into the open air. He went to the cabin where he had spent the night, and took his blankets and gear. His pony was in the corral waiting for him as he approached, and when he had mounted, Ted rode to the big gate. Not a soul was in sight, for every man in the place wanted to hear the story of the massacre. Ted managed to raise the great bar and open the gate. He led the pony outside and mounted again.

He rode slowly for a while, until he was out of sight of the fort, then he let the horse have its head, to travel its own pace, for the rider was too heartsick to care where he went so long as he went far from the company of murderers. He rode for hours, head on his chest, heedless of the dozens of skeletons and graves he passed. When, he asked himself, would law and order come to the territories? When would it be safe for honest men to build homesteads and have their wives and families with them on this great frontierland? He was sure that it would not be good to have his mother out of Edmonton yet. But perhaps his father and René and himself could get started on the farm. The land around Spitzee had seemed peaceful enough.

He rode on through the rest of the day, camped, and rode on for another day, until he approached the crossing in the valley of Spitzee. When he reached the river he did not stop, but crossed the stream and climbed the north bank. He turned into the old trail and headed back to Edmonton.

Chapter Six

A HALF-HOUR'S ride from the river brought Ted out on the open plain again, and he halted. Far to the north his eyes caught a slight puff of smoke on the horizon. He watched it for several minutes, and when it was followed by several other puffs, he took special notice of its location. It seemed to come from some place more to the east than the trail would take him, probably far across the river, but he knew it was Indian, and very possibly enemy. There was little wind at this time of the day. The round puffs rose high into the air before they disappeared. Ted could not read the signals but he knew that it was some kind of warning or alert, and might spell trouble for an unwary traveller. He turned off the trail and headed toward the long low hill that the Indians called Sitook Spagway, "the middle heights".

His eyes and ears were ever tuned to the world around him, on the alert for any hostile sign or sound, not only in the air and along the horizon, but on the ground ahead of him as well. He was almost into the rises of the heights when the signal billowed up in front of him. It was another smoke, this time from the very hills toward which he was heading. He pulled the pony to a stop and let it graze while he thought.

In front of him was the tiny creek that his Stony friends had called Flag Tongue. Somewhere nearby, he knew, the Indians were camping, but how many, and what tribe, he did not know. He rode very carefully up the creek for a little distance, until he was close to the place where he had seen the signal. He dismounted and led his pony into a little coulee branching off from the creek, and tied the animal to a willow. Then he started creeping up the bank and along the creek, watching for any sign of the Indians.

By watching the edge of the hill he could see a blue cloud of smoke some distance ahead of him, so he crept toward it. A sound made him freeze where he lay, and very slowly he lowered his body into the grass, lying as still as the rocks around him. His ear pressed against the ground told him nothing, for it was too far to feel the footfalls of moccasins. Presently, as he lay still, there came to his nostrils the scent of fire, and then he was able to pick out the odour of buckskin.

After a few moments he eased forward again, only a few feet, and lay motionless. Again he sniffed, and again the breeze bore him the smell of buckskin. In a few moments he inched forward again, and in a strained moment caught the sound of voices. He lay for some time listening, but could not catch the words to tell whether the Indians were friends or foes.

He decided to risk another crawl to try to make sure.

With each foot he moved forward he could hear more clearly the voices of the campers, but they did not speak any language he could recognize. They were neither English, French nor Stony. So intent on his listening was he that he moved almost automatically along the ground. He came to the edge of the bank so suddenly that he almost rolled over and down into the creek bottom.

Had he done so, he would have certainly fallen right on top of the Indians, for their fire was right below him. He froze where he lay at the edge of the rock, not daring to stir lest their keen eyes detect movement against the sharp outline of the creek bank. There were five of them, all bucks. Blackfoot! Ted knew that he must go back and get as far away as possible, for of all the tribes on the plains, the Blackfoot were the most feared.

When none of the men below were looking his way, he carefully lowered his head and shoulders below the edge of rock. Any quick movement would have been noticed, so it took nearly ten minutes before he felt it was safe enough to move faster. He pushed himself backward a few inches, feeling his way with hands and toes. As he crawled, he felt his thigh brush past a large stone. Slowly, ever so slowly, he inched back down the slope, gripping the large rock to keep from going too fast. As he slid past, he felt the stone move under his grip, and suddenly it came loose. Before he could hold it and push it back into its hole again, the round rock rolled free and went bounding down the slope. Instantly Ted froze again. He lay in the long grass of the stony hillside, listening to the noise of the rolling stone.

For a few seconds there was no sound to be heard. The Indians had stopped talking and Ted knew they were listening. Then came the soft pad of a footfall nearby, and the hiding boy was sure that the whole party was creeping around, looking for whatever had made the noise. Ted held his breath, and hoped that the pounding of his heart could not be heard. There came another whisper of a moccasined foot close beside him, and he drew himself closer to the ground.

Suddenly he heard a great shout from the man, and he winced and closed his eyes as he felt the sudden blast of the gun that roared toward him. But even as the rifle exploded, he felt rather than heard the frenzied whirr of feathers not two feet from him, and the grouse lifted on booming wings and soared over him. Then came the coughing curse of the Indian, for he had missed a perfect shot. The bird had startled the native, and in his excitement he must have missed seeing the still form in the grass, for the next moment brought a pounding of feet as the Indian raced downhill after the bird. Ted lay where he was, listening to the cries of the other Indians, and soon the air was still again.

The Indians had run upstream, so Ted was certain they had not noticed his horse. He found that his face and back were soaking wet, which was not caused entirely by the sun overhead. He waited a little while longer, until he was sure the racket had died away and his horse was still safe; then he began his slow crawl back to the pony.

He took the haltershank from the willow and, leading the horse, walked some distance downstream, where he crossed the creek a thousand yards below the Indian camp. Then he led the pony nearly half a mile farther into the hills and mounted. As he rode on into the hilly land of the heights he kept his eyes open wider than ever, and within a few minutes he crossed the trail of the Blackfoot party. That they were definitely Blackfoot he had no doubt, for there in the dust of the trail were the moccasin prints where they had dismounted for some reason. The prints showed clearly the design of the moccasin, and Ted could be certain of the tribe that wore it. He tried to judge where the trail led, and it seemed to head directly toward the place where the five natives had camped. They had come out of the northwest, and the boy felt no need to worry any more about that particular party. He put them out of his mind, but kept watch for any other humans who might be abroad on the prairies.

He stayed down in the lower land as he moved northward, following the gulleys wherever possible, so that any riders that might approach would show up against the skyline, while he himself would have a good chance of remaining undetected.

It was late afternoon when Ted came out of the Spagway country. As he looked out over the prairie that lay before him, he saw the line of trees in the distance, and realized that he was not far from the crossing called Okotoks. And straight ahead was the biggest rock that he had ever seen away from the mountains.

The rock lay all alone in the prairie, perhaps a mile from the river and trees. It appeared to be a great boulder broken in half, for one huge slab lay almost buried while the other piece stood up at least thirty feet above the ground. Its face was scored by numerous cracks that made it look like the face of an old Indian. They looked big enough to crawl into, and if so, Ted thought, they would make fine places to hide from enemy eyes. Accordingly he headed for the rock, making sure that no one was in sight to watch him. As he approached it, the rock seemed even larger than it had looked from the hills. The great crack which divided the larger piece was quite large enough for a man to crawl into, and Ted climbed from his pony and explored.

It was a fine place, this stone. Cracks ran in all directions across the surface, making tunnels and paths that led right into the centre of the stone, and there Ted found that the rock was split again lengthways, making a narrow passage-way right into the heart of the mass. This fissure was large enough to ride a horse into, so Ted rushed back to his mount and led it around to the west side of the rock, and up the narrow slit to the hollow centre. The horse was completely hidden from outside eyes, for the smaller half of the stone lay directly in front of the entrance to the crevice, and the walls on all sides were twenty feet high. When the pony was concealed and looked after, Ted went outside and brushed away all traces of tracks leading to the rock and into the crevice. He picked out a level slab of rock for his bed, and settled down with some dried meat for his supper.

Ted lay all night on stone, sleeping fitfully in the quiet, for there were no trees to sigh, or streams to burble, and even the coyotes seemed to be silent around the rock. From time to time the horse stamped or snuffled or snorted, but no other sound broke the stillness. What a wonderful place to hide, he thought. Why, from here a man could look out all across the countryside, even across the little river to the north. And even if a hostile Indian or trader came near, he could not possibly see a man lying on top of the stone, or his horse in the crevice. He fell asleep thinking of the possibilities of this stone.

It was early morning when he woke. Through a tiny slit above him he could see the dark sky. The stars had gone, but the sun was barely above the eastern horizon. Even though the air was cold, Ted could feel the warmth of the newborn sun already. He lay still for a while, thinking again of how he might hide in this place indefinitely, within earshot of the Blackfeet if they should happen to pass on the trail to the crossing of Okotoks. His eyes roamed around the small room where he lay, and in the wakening dawn he could see the great slabs of stone that had fallen to form this chamber. As he looked at them, he gave a start and sat bolt upright. There could be no mistake.

He stared all around him then, looking carefully at the walls of this rude shelter. "This," he thought to himself, "is no place for me to stay." For the coloured drawings on the rocks were the crude picture-writings of Indians, done in that red paint they used. On all sides of the crevice were the pictures, and though Ted did not know what they meant, he knew they spelled Indian and Indian might spell trouble if it was Blackfoot. So he had guessed wrong about this rock. Instead of being a haven of refuge, it seemed to be some kind of sacred place that drew Indians from their camps and trails. There he was, right in the middle of Blackfoot country and in the middle of one of their sacred places. It was time to get going.

Ted had no quarrel with the Blackfoot Nation; indeed, he had met very few men of that tribe. But then, the Blackfeet did not know Ted either, and anyone who travelled across their land was likely to be stopped. It was common knowledge that some tribes of the Blackfoot Nation were the most warlike Indians on the plains, and from the many stories he had heard, Ted had built up a healthy respect for them. Not that he was afraid of them, for by this time he felt that he could meet any man on equal terms; but he had found that the best way to handle trouble was to avoid it. He knew that the best thing to do was to get on his horse and ride as fast as possible away from the rock.

With great haste he got to his feet and scrambled out of the tiny hole where he had spent the night. His pony was where he had left it and was beginning to become restless. But before he could mount, he heard voices. Silently he stepped back into his crevice and listened. In a moment came the rustling of clothing against leather and the sound of unshod horses. Poking his head between two slabs, he peered cautiously out, and a moment later the Indians came into view.

They were the five scouts from whom he had escaped the day before; and they were looking for trouble, to judge by their paint. Ted had guessed wrong about them, too— they had not continued south as he had expected. They had doubled back, possibly on his trail, and now barred his way to freedom. He wondered if they *had* found his trail, but then reasoned that if they had, they would not now be acting so calmly.

While he lay watching, they halted a few paces from the rock and dismounted. Two of them began to gather material for a fire. No doubt they had been on the trail since before sunup, and were stopping for a morning meal. Another Indian took the ponies' ropes and led the animals to an outcropping of stone, to tie them. Another walked down the length of the stone and disappeared around the corner; and Ted felt a thrill of near panic go through him. What if the fellow discovered his horse!

The boy fought down a desire to rush out and try to get away, but common sense told him it would be no use, for they had their ponies close and also weapons. He looked around his prison, thinking of all the ways he might escape. Could he climb to the top of the rock and wait above the crevice to jump on the man if he found the horse? Then he could be away before they knew what was happening. But suppose he killed the man, or he made an outcry? No, that was not the way. There must be some other idea.

Would it be possible, he wondered, for him just to climb into the rock and stay there, even though they did find the horse? Hardly, he told himself. After all, these men knew the rock better than he. They could starve him out, or trap him in it. Clearly, the only way out seemed to lead upward, to the top.

He started to climb up the jagged crevice where he had spent the night, and found that the going was quite easy, for the broken slabs made fine hand- and footholds. As silently as he knew how, he pulled himself upward, and in a little while he reached the top. It was a bright, clear day, and from his place on the stone he could look out over the whole countryside, even down through the trees to the river. He could hear clearly the Indian voices as they talked among themselves; and then, even as he drew himself up out of the crack, he heard the yell that told of the discovery of his horse.

There came such a gabble of sound and shouts, then silence fell. Ted knew they were listening and planning. In the quietness every tiny noise could be heard, and the scream of a hawk miles away reached his ears.

Could he, he wondered, climb back down that cliff, right into their camp, and ride off with their horses, as he had done when he was only a child? With this plan in mind he began to inch his way back into the crevice. The solidly packed stones gave him good support as he lowered himself, and no metal or hard leather was on his clothing to give any sound that might betray him. Bit by bit he went down, and soon was in position to peer over the rock right into the camp. There was not a man in sight, either below him or anywhere around. They were all inside the rock, or around the corner. The horses stood where they had been tethered, munching noisily on a dry bush.

Ted began the descent of the last part of the rock. From the other side came a rustle as clothing scraped against stone, and he could hear one of the searchers breathing heavily. Below him Ted could see that there was a drop of only ten feet to the ground, and a twenty-foot run to the horses. Without a sound he began to edge over the rock and let himself down, hanging tightly by both hands. He dropped his full length past the place where he had spent the night, and with his feet searched for a hold. And as he hung there, he felt two hard bare arms circle his waist, holding him so that he could go neither up nor down.

In an instant another pair of hands quickly looped a length of rawhide thong about his wrists, and flipped his hands from their clutch on the rock above. He fell heavily in the sand at the base of the rock, and before he could regain his breath, he was buried under howling, naked bodies. Though there were actually only three men who jumped on him, they seemed to Ted like at least a dozen, to judge by the noise they set up. One Indian grabbed his bound hands and jerked him to a sitting position; another grasped his belt and heaved him to his feet. He felt the sharp point of some weapon thrust against his back, and over the mad screaming of the three captors, heard the yells of the other two as they scrambled to the scene.

They almost dragged him to the place where they had

started their fire, and he was shoved to the ground, tied hand and foot, and then completely ignored while the five warriors ate the bit of dried meat they had seared over the tiny fire. Ted could not understand much of their talk, for he did not know the Blackfoot language, but at times he could make out names and words that he recognized.

One word he heard them repeat several times was "Okotoks". That was what the Stonies had called the place where the trail crossed this little stream just to the north. They must have been planning to go there. But he said nothing, did nothing except what he was directly ordered to do. When they had finished their meagre meal, they put him on his pony and tied him there with more leather thongs. Then they mounted, with Ted in the middle of the file, his horse led by one of the Indians. They moved directly toward the line of trees that bordered the river.

Chapter Seven

T ED realized that the Blackfeet were taking him to their main camp, and he wondered what might be in store for him when they arrived. He remembered the stories told at Edmonton, how these plains' Blackfeet were the wildest and most warlike nation in the whole West. As he bounced from side to side he could only hope that his training would help to keep him from crying out when they began their torture, for he knew that to show any sign of pain would make him a coward in their eyes and perhaps lead to further abuse, while a silent endurance might induce them to grant him a quick death.

The dust of the prairie rolled from under them as they raced along the trail, and suddenly out of the brown cloud appeared two more riders. When the newcomers saw him they gave great whoops of joy, and Ted could guess the entertainment they planned to have that night. Just then they came in sight of the camp, and the whole band seemed to be on hand to greet him. One of the scouts must have ridden ahead to tell the news, for as they rode into the camp they were greeted with loud cries and laughter.

What bothered Ted most was the crowd of women and children that clustered close around his horse when they stopped in the camp. He was too tired and sore even to try to understand what was said among the men, but one of the leaders gave some sort of command and at his word the entire camp broke into howls of glee, and Ted felt himself swaying as hands clutched him and grabbed at his clothing. His feet were still tied under the horse's belly so that he could not kick out at his tormentors, but suddenly the thong that bound his ankles was cut and he began to slide. Hands clutched his legs, even though he tried to kick free of them; hands caught at his leggings and jacket, and hands grasped his shirt. He fell then, and heard his shirt tear as it was ripped from neck to waist. And as suddenly as he had fallen, a hush came over the crowd near him. He half lay, half sat, on the ground, and the circle closed around him. For a moment or two he looked at the faces above him, seeing the staring eyes and open mouths. Then the young men and the boys stepped back, forcing the others with them, and the shrilling of the squaws was stilled. Ted got to his feet, and the press about him lessened as the crowd fell back even farther. One or two of the squaws began to jabber then, very softly and, it seemed, almost reverently.

Then the circle was broken by an old, wrinkled Indian, who stepped forward to stand in front of Ted. The white boy looked directly into the grey eyes of this man; then the Indian's glance moved from Ted's face to his chest. Ted looked down, noting for the first time that his torso was bare, and suddenly he knew what had stopped the crowd. The tearing of his shirt had revealed the necklace.

The old man reached out a hand and touched the claws, and he spoke in Blackfoot. Ted shook his head and said a few words in English, then in Stony. At the English the old man frowned, but when he heard the Stony he uttered an exclamation, then shouted something that was answered from outside the circle.

In a few moments a warrior elbowed his way through the throng, pushing a man ahead of him. The old Blackfoot said something to this man, who then turned to Ted and spoke in Stony.

"I am a Stony," he said, "and I speak for this great chief, Battle Drum, who is head of this band of Blackfoot warriors. He asks who you are, and by what right you wear the claws of the great mountain bear."

"Tell him," replied Ted, "that I am a traveller who comes in peace and wishes to pass in peace. As for the claws, I took them from the feet of the great devil bear."

"And did you kill this bear yourself?"

"I killed the bear with my rifle. He had stolen my meat. I trailed him to his den and shot him and took his hide and claws."

At these words the Stony became much excited, jabbering so fast that Ted could not understand him. "The hide, the robe——" he spluttered finally, "what did you do with it?"

"The robe I gave to my adopted father, Many Horses, who is of the band of Broken Shield. It is they whom I have come to find, but they are not here." Ted wondered if this man could tell him of the Stony band he sought. But he did not ask.

"This story is true!" exclaimed the Stony. "I myself saw this robe, and heard the song of the great devil bear who was killed by a brave white hunter." His eyes shone with pride as he turned to the Blackfoot chief and translated what had been said. So enthusiastic was his description that even the old chief's eyes wrinkled with belief. He ripped out an order, and the children, who had packed themselves around the white man, rolled and stumbled back. The squaws ran helter-skelter to their labours, and soon only the elders of the band, and the Stony, were left.

Ted stood quietly as the Indians talked among themselves. Suddenly one of the men drew a long knife from his breechcloth and advanced to where Ted stood. The white boy did not know what to expect, but he drew himself up as straight as he could, and waited. The knife flashed briefly, and Ted's hands were free. He stared at them for a moment, then at the Indians, and he laughed in sheer relief. The Indians did not smile in return, but their look was more friendly. Then the Stony spoke.

"These Blackfeet have decided that you are to be free to move about the camp, but like me you must remain in the village and work as a slave. If you try to escape, you will be killed. But do not be sad. This band is very rich. They have many horses, and they kill many buffalo. You will always have enough to eat, and plenty of fine robes to keep you warm, and a good tepee to shelter you. It is not a bad life, except that captives must work all day with the women." He sighed, and his look of disgust made Ted's lips twitch.

"I will not stay in this camp if I find that I can get away," he told the Stony as they walked toward the tents.

"Nor I," replied the other. He led the white boy to a

skin-covered lodge near the centre of the camp, explaining that this was the tepee that was to be Ted's home with the Blackfeet. The two captives were to share it.

Ted noticed that his pony had been taken to a group of horses near the edge of the camp, and he was surprised to see that they were held together only by a thin rope of rawhide stretched in a sort of corral from tree to tree. The animals had been so well trained that even the lightest rope would serve to hold them inside. He ducked his head and stepped through the door of the tent.

"I do not think they will make you work as hard as the rest of us," said the Stony, who now introduced himself as Night Walker. "They hold your trophy as very great medicine, and are almost afraid of you."

"I guess the necklace is big medicine in all tribes, is it not?" asked Ted.

"Yes," grunted the other. "It is the sign of the bravest hunter, and bravery is the passport in Blackfoot country. I only wish that I were half so brave."

"Well, if it will only get me out of this camp and on my pony again and headed toward Edmonton, I'll figure it was worth the risk I took getting it," Ted sighed. "I sure hate losing my pony and my old rifle."

"They will give you back your rifle," said Night Walker.

"What!" Ted could not believe it.

"Without powder or shot," finished the Indian, smiling a little as Ted moaned at the disappointment.

"But what will they do with me?" the lad asked, after a pause.

"They will probably make you promise not to run away, and after a few years you may wish to join the tribe and become one of them. They need good hunters, and you would be welcome when they go to trade with the white men."

"Oho!" Ted thought, "so that's their game! Well, we'll just see about that. I intend to get away as soon as I can, and I'll bet there's not an Indian in the territories who'll catch me when I do. If I could only get word to White Calf——"

"White Calf—my Indian brother—do you know where he is?" he asked.

"White Calf?" the other man shrugged. "I do not know of any White Calf."

"But you must!" cried Ted—and then he realized that there was little chance for this to be so, for Indians change names several times as they grow up, and very probably White Calf was called something else now.

"He is the son of Many Horses, of the band of Broken Shield," Ted explained desperately. "You said that you had seen the robe I gave to Many Horses. Tell me what you know of this family."

"I know little of the band of Broken Shield," admitted the Stony. "It is true that I passed through their camp many moons ago, and that I saw the robe of the great bear, but I do not know where they have gone, or who was in the band."

"But don't you know where they were heading when you met them?"

"Broken Shield and his band were heading for the great shining hills. They went to hunt there, for the buffalo have gone from the plains now."

Ted was sorry to hear this news. The buffalo had supplied nearly everything that an Indian family needed to live, and now that they were fast disappearing, he knew that his friends would have much trouble finding food enough and clothing to keep warm.

"Too bad!" he said. "I wish I could help them."

"You had better think of helping yourself, if you wish to escape from this camp," said the Stony. "I will help you if I can, but if I am caught, I will die."

Ted thanked him, then sat thinking deeply of what the morrow might bring.

Just before dark the flap of the tepee was flung open and a large bowl of hot meat and vegetables was shoved inside. And with the bowl came Ted's rifle, in its case, and also his worn buckskin hunting pouch. His belt with knife, powder flask and shot bag was with it. The flask and shot bag were empty, but the little box which held his caps was there, and still full. The Indians knew that he could not do much damage with only caps.

When they had eaten their fill of the good stew, the two new friends sat back in the dark tent and talked of their future in the camp; and when they grew sleepy, they rolled in soft warm buffalo robes.

Ted awoke to a bustle of activity in the Blackfoot camp, and for a little while could not remember where he was. But when he realized his position, he crawled out of the robes. Not a moment too soon, either, for a head poked through the flaps and an arm waved him to come out. The sun was hardly peeking through the trees as he joined the rest of the camp, squatting by one of the many fires for his morning meal. This was quite a treat for Ted, having his breakfast served to him; but it was only the first day. From then on he had to be up and working before the others, for he was a captive and must work for his food. He was treated much like the other prisoners in the camp, of whom there were several, all from different tribes and none speaking either English or Stony.

Part of Ted's job was to help the women gather vegetables. It was from these wise old women that he learned about the bountiful food supply that grew in the woods and on the plains all around him. They led him each morning into the forest along the river, and he collected the various roots and herbs that they pointed out to him. He memorized everything he could, and watched carefully as the squaws prepared each plant, drying or cooking or mixing with other things. There were so many different kinds of plants that were good to eat that Ted could only wonder that he had come so close to starving when he had lived in the mountains. Although meat was the main diet of these people too, they knew all the plants that would make the meat supply last longer, and fill out the meals properly.

The Indians used almost everything that grew. Some of the roots, when boiled or baked properly, turned into the most delicious food Ted had eaten, and some, when pounded, could be made into a sort of flour that was baked into wonderful little cakes. Some of the herbs were not eaten, but were dried and used as magical charms, while still others could be boiled to produce the brilliant dyes with which the Indians coloured their garments and painted their faces.

How Ted wished he had known of this back in the mountains! Here was everything that man needed, he thought—food and medicine and paints, and even fibres that could be made into clothing. He dug the bulbous, pulpy roots that grew near water, he learned how to bake the fleshy roots of many flowers, and to boil and grind others into flour and meal. Even the tobacco that the chiefs smoked was gathered from the fields, when white man's tobacco was not to be had.

Even in the late summer the bushes were loaded with berries, many of them dried up, but still good when boiled with other things, or mashed into a bag of pemmican. The subject of pemmican was something that worried Ted, for these Indians made very little of the greasy, life-preserving mixture. From his Stony friend he learned that some bands were too lazy to make their own pemmican, but preferred to buy their supplies from other bands who were better at the job than they. Horses were the main item of trade, and it looked as though this band would be able to lay in quite a supply when the time came.

But then the thought came to him that all might not be well this year. He had learned that the buffalo were gone from the grasslands; and buffalo was the main part of the pemmican. Suppose the Indians who made the pemmican could not get their supply of meat this year? What would the Blackfoot band do? He thought more and more about this, but said nothing, hoping only that he would be gone long before he needed to face the problem.

Chapter Eight

Iɴ the days that followed his capture by the Blackfeet, Ted came to know them quite well and even began to learn a little of their language. He found that he already knew a few words, for many of the names used by his Stony friends were actually Blackfoot names that had been applied to the rivers and hills in this part of the West many years before the Stonies had moved to the foothill country. He learned that the very name of his valley, Spitzee, was really a Blackfoot word meaning "the crossing of the river where the trees grow tall", just as it meant in Stony; only these people called it Is-pit-zee.

The great boulder where Ted had been captured was called Okotoks, for in Blackfoot that meant "big rock". And this crossing of the small stream had come to be called Okotoks also, for he knew that important places on the prairie were named for the most distinguishing feature close by them.

Ted studied his captors all day long while he was with them, and he learned that the Blackfoot Nation was a proud, fierce warrior nation, ever ready to defend honour and avenge wrongs done to it. For many years—in fact, longer than even the oldest member of the tribe could re-member—they had been fighting a ceaseless war with the Crees. It was a not infrequent occurrence for the younger, more hot-blooded braves to stir themselves to frenzy with a wild war dance, then leap on their ponies and ride madly off into the hills or plains, howling their desire to spill Cree blood.

The older men approved of these displays, and encour-aged and fed the age-old hatred of their enemy. In this way they knew that there would always be a reserve of enmity for the Crees, even after the present leaders had passed on.

The young bloods would ride away screaming their taunts and threats to the four winds; but more often than not the party would return the next morning, cooled down by their ride, hungry and tired. Yet they were looked upon with pride and affection by their fathers, and all the band cheered them for their spirit and their eagerness to uphold the traditions of their nation.

Were the Blackfeet also enemies of the Stonies, Ted wondered. If so, why did they allow a tiny band of Stonies to live in the Spitzee valley, right in the heart of Blackfoot territory, without being raided and chased away? The next night, when he again got a chance to speak with Night Walker, Ted called softly to him and the two sat close in their tent.

"Tell me, Stony friend," said Ted, "are the Blackfeet also at war with the Assiniboines? And do they fight?"

"Yes, white brother, the Blackfeet and Assiniboines are

at war, although it is not so strong as between the Blackfeet and the Crees. My people are very few, but our warriors are brave and strong, and make many raids on the Blackfeet. That is why the Blackfeet do not like us. We steal all their horses, for it is well known that of all the tribes on the prairies, the Blackfeet are the richest, and have the most horses. And a Blackfoot without a horse is like a buffalo without feet.

"It is the same way with my people. We need our horses, and that is why we capture them from the Blackfeet. Wherever the Blackfeet go, my people know where to find them, and even now this camp may be watched by scouts from my band, or the band of Broken Shield. But we must not hope too strongly. It may not be so. Yet we must be ready if the Stonies do come."

"I'm ready right now," said Ted in an excited whisper. "I could jump on a horse and ride off without even thinking about it."

"Good!" replied Night Walker. "Now we must sleep, for we must work again on the morrow. Say no more, or they will hear us and think we are planning to escape." The two men lay on their robes, and Ted fell asleep thinking of what to do if the raid came that night.

But the raid did not come. The days passed, and Ted observed the lives of the Blackfeet. The women cooked and sewed and pounded and scraped, all the while caring for the younger children; and the men hunted a little, ate a lot, and slept a good part of the time. Even though the countryside seemed peaceful, a lookout was kept at all times, for the chief knew that his herd of ponies would be a great prize to any wandering war party. Ted tried to keep himself in readiness without showing his impatience and anxiety. But with all his preparedness, he was not ready when the raid really came.

The first sign came on a day late in the summer, near dusk. Thunder growled over the storm-clouded foothills as the lookout gave the alarm. Ted heard the howl of the coyote, and the chorus that came after, but he had heard coyotes so many times that he did not even take notice of the noise. Suddenly he became aware that the whole camp was moving, bustling with activity. Within moments came the second cry from far away, echoing along the river banks. Ted heard the excited, urgent voices of the Indians, though he could not understand what was being said; and he knew that trouble must be coming. Perhaps another flood, like the one at Spitzee, for it was raining heavily to the west, and they had camped in a low place. He watched the people, moving closer to see what was going on.

Almost before he knew it, the warriors had gone. They had leaped on their ponies and simply disappeared into the dusk. Behind them they left the old men, women, children and a large number of horses. Ted saw his own pony among those that milled around inside the rope corral, and he walked quickly over to the animals. Now was his chance. The men had all gone away, and here was his horse, and he was left unguarded.

As he paused for a moment at the corral, trying to decide on the best way to escape, the prick of a sharp object made him jump. He turned to look into the cold eyes of an old man. An iron-tipped arrow, drawn full length across the bow, was aimed directly at him. Ted did not understand the fellow's words, but he understood enough to turn away from the horses and walk back to his own tent. The guard followed him all the way, and did not lower his weapon until Ted stepped up to the door flap. Ted's back was to the camp when the Stonies struck.

They came out of the dark west, out of the night, moving so swiftly and silently that even the old Blackfoot did not see or hear them until they were in the middle of the camp and moving out again, driving the horses before them. Somehow they had managed to draw off the fighting men of the camp, sneak on foot right into the corral, each choose a horse, mount and drive away the entire herd, all without being seen by any of the Blackfoot women or children. Before Ted could make a sound, the raiders were gone, roaring away into the thunderstorm that enveloped the camp and the valley.

The Stonies had used an old trick. They had waited until the storm struck, and then made good their escape, knowing that the torrents of water from the cloudburst would soon wash away all trace of their trail and they would be free to drive the horses anywhere for several days without fear of being overtaken.

It had happened so fast that Ted was stunned. All his plans had been wasted. He dived into the tent, calling, "Night Walker! Night Walker! They came! They've gone!" But no answer came from the dark tent. Night Walker had gone too!

For the rest of the night the Blackfeet talked of the raid, and in the morning the braves came back. They did not howl or scream now. A few rode, but most of the party walked. They did not sing brave songs, or yell defiance. The homecoming party was only half as large as the party that went out.

The squaws sang. They sang their songs of grief for their men who would not come back. The Stonies had planned an ambush and the Blackfoot party had been scattered, pulled from their mounts so that the horses would not be injured, and some of the men killed. Most of them had been set afoot by the swift-moving raiders.

Ted felt a great relief at the news, although he heard that some of the attackers had been killed in the battle. But the Stonies had got away with all but a dozen horses. What they could not capture they had killed under the Blackfoot riders. They had struck like the lightning that flashed over the scene, and had vanished as quickly; and there was no hope of following in the face of the blinding fury of the rain.

All morning the women kept up their wails, even as they went about the regular chores of the camp. When the dead Blackfeet were brought in, the weeping and moaning increased. Ted noticed one old crone whose hand was covered with blood; but the injury seemed not to bother her, for she took no notice of it as she worked. Then he saw that many of the other women had wounds too—and all on the hands.

It was not until midday that he found out the reason. Each hand that bled lacked a finger, some of them even two. Then he was horrified as he watched a squaw lay a finger on a log and actually strike it off with a large knife. Ted knew that some of the dead Blackfeet had been in her family; and then he realized the truth. Every woman who had lost a husband or son cut off a finger in grief. The sight stayed in his mind long after they had buried the fallen warriors.

Ted watched the funeral with awe. Unlike the Stonies, who laid their dead on platforms in the trees, the Blackfeet carried the bodies to the highest part of the river bank, overlooking the most beautiful part of the valley, and laid them on the grass, setting beside them their favourite weapons and trappings. Around them they built circles of stones to represent tents, and one important man was laid inside a real tepee. Ted remembered the rings and tents he had seen on the hills near Whoop Up. He had been told that sometimes the Blackfeet even burned the bodies and built cairns of stones above them. The cries of the mourning women rose higher and higher as the rites progressed, and when the ceremony was finished, the Indians filed back into camp.

Shortly before nightfall Ted was lying in his tent thinking about the day's activities when the flap was roughly pushed aside and a young Indian entered. He spoke to Ted, but the white youth shook his head. He did not understand. The other spoke the name of the chief and waved Ted outside. They walked across the silent camp to the big tepee of Battle Drum.

Ted stepped through the opening as he was bidden by his escort, and in the gloom he saw the chief on the far side, enthroned on a deep pile of furs. Beside him were several other men. The chief gazed unblinking at the white boy for a while, and not a sound broke the still air. Then Battle Drum turned to the man nearest him and spoke rapidly. The other grunted and addressed Ted in halting English.

"Our great chieftain, Battle Drum, asks that you speak with him. He——" and here the native could go no farther in English, but changed to a mixture of Stony and Blackfoot and English. Ted could follow the sense of it, which was something like this:

"He bids me tell you that we of his band wish to make

peace with the white hunter who has killed the great mountain bear. He says that now all in this camp must work together to live, for without our horses we cannot hunt or move. We have little food, and nothing with which to buy from our friends. All our good hunters have been killed. My chief asks that you come with your mighty thunder stick and help us kill meat so that we may live for yet another winter."

"Tell your chief that I will give him my word to help in the hunt," Ted told the man in slow Stony, making sure that the other understood. When this message had been relayed to the chief, a sudden smile wrinkled his face. Why, thought Ted, he looks almost human.

"Tell him I make peace with this band of the Blackfoot Nation," he added.

A long, red-bowled pipe was lighted and Ted watched as it was passed to the chief. The Indian placed the end in his mouth and drew a long puff. He then pointed the stem to the four corners of the tepee, towards the four main compass points, and breathed out a cloud of queer-smelling smoke. The pipe was passed to Ted, and the young man did his best to follow exactly the actions of the Indian. When all in the tent had saluted the four winds, they rose and the meeting was over.

Shortly after Ted reached his tepee again, one of the braves brought him his powder and shot. He sat down, cleaned his rifle carefully, and with a feeling of great satisfaction loaded it.

Ted's first kill next day was a fat deer, several miles up the creek. The Indians went wild with delight when he brought it down, and it did not take them long to drag it back to camp, skin, cut up and cook it. And it took them even less time to eat it. Ted was amazed at the speed with which these fellows cleaned up the whole carcass. If they had not brought in another animal themselves the same day, some of the women would have gone hungry, for after the braves had eaten their fill, the squaws could finish what was left. As it was, there was not much left by the end of the second day, and Ted spent the whole of the next day on the plain without even sighting an animal. The Indians bagged a few rabbits and birds that day, but the game was growing wary.

The large camp had been in the valley for many weeks, and the wildlife in the nearby area was becoming depleted. Without the horses that were left, they would not have been able to bring in half the meat they did. And soon the last of the deer had been killed within a day's march in all directions. Even the hunters who went out on the ponies could not get enough meat to supply more than a mouthful for each person.

On the sixth day after the raid, they killed a horse and ate that. Ted began to realize the struggle to survive that followed such a raid as the Stonies had made. He was obliged to fight for his life, never knowing from one day to the next if he would eat or go hungry. How different it was to his life in the mountains! There he had only himself to look after, the hills were full of game, and one kill would last him two weeks or more.

There was hardly a living thing in the valley of the Okotoks now, and what game could be shot was so far away from the camp that it was often eaten by the hunters before it could be taken back to the rest. Another horse met the same fate as the first, and now there were only ten left. The next day one pony was found dead, and for a day or two there was food in the village. Then when that was gone, there was nothing.

The young men were growing too weak from hunger to be able to venture far afield. One by one the horses disappeared into the cooking pots, and finally the day came when there was nothing at all to eat, save the rawhide haltershanks and pieces of clothing. These rubbery chunks of leather were boiled day and night, and the resulting broth was at least filling, if not nutritious. Soon they had chewed their way through most of the spare leather that lay about the camp, and one day Ted watched as the squaws fought for the slimy bits that were burned to the bottom of the pots.

For many years Ted would remember that day. When the last of the thin stew had been drained and scraped from the pots, the Indians simply sat around the fires, thinking of many things, and some of the older bucks began to sing their death songs. But the silence did not last long. It was broken by the pounding feet of a runner, and his long, breathless howl as he staggered into the camp. It was one of the young hunters who had ventured upriver that morning.

The lad dashed out of the woods, nearly running through one of the fires in his haste. At the top of his voice he screamed his message. Ted could not understand what was said, but on the instant every man, woman and child was dashing and yelling. Surely not another raid! Ted reached for his rifle and gear, determined not to miss the chance this time. But he paused when he noticed that, while the men took up their weapons, the women grabbed blankets and robes and sticks. Above the uproar Ted could pick out only one word in Blackfoot that he could understand. But that one word was enough to make him sling his rifle and pouch and belt over his shoulder and run with the rest. In Blackfoot they shouted and chanted the word: "Buffalo!"

Chapter Nine

BUFFALO!
The word spread like magic from mouth to mouth, and soon was being shouted all across the camp. A number of the younger Indians picked up whatever weapons they had and ran off in single file, heading up over the river bank onto the plain above. The rest of the camp went almost crazy. Although they were weak from hunger, the thought of food gave them energy. Dancing and howling, they waved bows and spears, and within a few minutes the whole band was moving upstream along the creek. Ted learned that the braves who had run away first had gone to try to get behind the herd and drive it closer to the camp.

Just how or where the slaughter would take place was a mystery to Ted. There was not a horse in the camp now, and how anyone could hunt buffalo without horses was more than he could imagine. As he ran he remembered the grand hunt with the Stonies, when he had killed his first buffalo and surprised his father and Corteau. They would not believe he was hunting buffalo on foot now. Indeed, he found it hard to believe himself.

He was panting and well out of breath before the leaders of the hunting party stopped. Why they halted soon became clear to the white boy, as he realized their plan. Here was a part of the river where the bank rose steeply, over fifty feet at one point; and here the stream ran some distance away from the bank, for the valley was wide and flat. Even before he could catch his breath he was given his orders.

"Go to the top of the bank, white brother," shouted the chief. Ted did not understand the words, but the motions were clear. Then the Indian who spoke English was beside him, explaining:

"You will see our people standing there with blankets and bows. You must stand in line with the others, and when the buffalo come, you must shoot as many as you can, but only those on the outside, so that their bodies will fall and form a wall and frighten the others into our trap here at the cliff. Our hunters will do the same. In this way the animals that are not shot will be driven over the cliff and to their deaths."

"What if they are not killed at the fall?" Ted asked.

"Some of the old men and boys are here at the bottom, ready to kill those that might escape. We will get as many as we can before they get away. Our best runners have gone to the herd and are even now driving it toward us. Hurry, get into your line so that there will be no hole in the wall."

Ted turned and ran up the steep bank, barely making it to the top before he was out of breath again. Once there he could see other figures, some squatting as they waited, others standing with hands shading their eyes, trying to catch the first sight of the coming herd.

They were spread out across the flat land in two long straight lines, with the far ends wide apart, and narrowing down to a small opening at the steepest part of the bank. This was the trap. The buffalo, stampeded by the runners behind them, would rush blindly on, heading directly for the waiting Indians on the plain. Then, when they were in the widest part of the V, all the squaws and old men and hunters forming the lines would leap suddenly to their feet and begin to wave blankets and make as much noise as possible. The buffalo, quick to avoid unknown danger, would shy away from the people as they rushed headlong toward their doom at the narrow end of the lines. Too late the leaders would sense the danger at the cliff, and their fellows would force them over the edge, only to follow under pressure of those behind.

Ted stationed himself near one end of the long line of Indians, and knelt as they told him to do. Then they waited, and everything was quiet. Only the sounds of nature could be heard. If the lead buffalo happened to see any movement ahead of them, they would turn away from the trap, and the chance would be lost. Every man, woman and child in the camp knew that, and there was not a move or sound from any part of the ambush. As Ted listened, he saw the squaw next him put her ear to the ground, and did so himself. He heard the low drumming of the hooves of the running herd. The buffalo were coming. It was only a matter of minutes before the cloud of dust was seen on the far rise, and Ted held his breath as the thundering animals struck the trap.

Then the roar of the herd was almost drowned in the racket of screeching and howling as both lines of natives leaped to their feet and began the grimmest dance of their lives. In the face of this sudden fence of screaming humanity the lead buffalo slowed, not understanding this turn of events. Then, pushed by those behind, they streamed on between the narrowing lines.

Ted steadied his rifle and lined upon a bull that showed signs of turning toward the lines, and as it came near, he fired. The sound of the shot seemed to release all the energy in the buffalo, and they broke from their steady run into a wild flood of flesh and bone. Ted reloaded as quickly as he knew how, but even so he was almost too late as another animal charged out of the dust, straight toward him.

It was hardly a hundred feet away, and his rifle was not yet primed, when a loud bang sounded from nearby. He glanced at the buffalo, and it had turned away from the noise, heading back toward the rest of the herd. Ted looked to see who had helped him, and discovered an old wrinkled squaw, with a blanket waving from both hands. She had no gun. As Ted watched, she raised the blanket again and brought it down with a sudden snap, and the report was like that of a small cannon. Then from all sides came the sharp explosions as the greater part of the herd came into the V, and for fifteen minutes the sound of Ted's rifle was drowned by the noise of snapping blankets wielded by scores of energetic women.

The hunters in the lines stood their ground, sending arrow after arrow into the raging mass of buffalo. Ted fired and loaded until he was afraid to load again, lest the heat of his barrel should explode the powder before he was ready to fire. By this time most of the herd had passed, and the people at the outer ends of the trap were turning toward the cliff. Ted scrambled after them, and dropped over the bank into a storm of dust, noise and dead beasts. He sat on a rock and watched as the last of the herd fell to death. Below them ran perhaps two dozen bloodstreaked Indians, carrying short spears or long knives.

As each beast fell to the sod, a man ran to it. If the animal struggled to gain its feet, a swift stroke of the knife would sever the jugular vein, or hamstring it so that it could be killed. Those animals that did manage to get up were attacked by the spearmen. Ted noted that the spears were in expert hands. He had never seen these weapons used before, and it came as a surprise to him to see that they were not thrown at the target, but rather used as long knives, and stabbed downwards without being released. The long iron points flashed and came out red, and the aim of the attackers was usually good. Few second thrusts were needed.

The slaughter was soon finished. It had taken hardly half an hour from the time the trap had been sprung, and now there were over fifty huge carcasses waiting to be skinned and cut up. This was woman's work, and the squaws made no complaint as they threw down the blankets and sticks they had used up above, and set to work with their bone and stone knives, and the few steel blades they owned.

Once again Ted was amazed at these natives. For weeks they had starved, and now they had plenty to last them for several months if they were careful and took the trouble to dry or smoke the meat. But instead of doing this, they cut off only the choicest parts, just as though in time of plenty, and carried hides and meat downstream to their camp, leaving the greater part of the meat to be fought over by coyotes and magpies.

There was a regular party in camp that night. For the first time in weeks stomachs were full. Every brown face wore a smile of contentment, and Ted was told that the killing was regarded as an omen of good fortune, that the luck of the camp was changing for the better.

All the next day the celebration continued, and Ted could tell that some kind of sports display was shaping up because the younger men were taking short runs about the camp, and even boys were wrestling and playing games of physical skill. Although it was close to winter, no snow had fallen and the grass was brown, the ground was dry and hard. On the second day after the buffalo run the contests began.

Chapter Ten

TED was not sure just what to expect the next morning. He awoke very early, long before sunrise, and for a little while just lay in his robes, wondering at the noise and excitement outside. He knew it was to be a special day, and that there would be feasting and celebration, but he did not know what sort of activity had been planned. From some distance away came occasional shouts and howls of laughter, and he recognized the voices of some of the youngsters, evidently already well on the way to having a good time. When he finally stuck his head outside, the camp was bustling with preparations, and wonderful smells of cooking meat rose on all sides. Not much of the big hunt would be left after this day, he thought, and he meant to get his share of the food before it was all gone.

He wandered through the camp, watching the Indians as they went about their chores—the squaws cooking, and cleaning hides of the buffalo that had been killed; the men painting themselves and planning the day's activities. It did not take Ted long to find out what was to happen. First on the list was a feast. The whole band sat around the cooking fires and ate as much as each could hold; and as the last man staggered away, the sun rose and drove away the last shadows of night.

With the bright daylight came the warmth of the late fall sunshine, and soon the boys of the camp were gathered in a large group at one side of the area. Ted followed, willing to learn what he could. He did not quite follow the quick conversation of the Blackfoot boys, but he made out what appeared to be something to do with 'throwing the okotoks'. Okotoks! That was what his captors had called the big rock where he had been captured, and what this crossing at the river was named. He soon found out that any large stone was an okotoks, and that throwing it was a popular game with these boys. Ted watched with much amusement as the Indian lads lined up and one after another tried their hands at the sport. It was a competition to see who could throw the big stones the farthest, backwards, between the legs.

Each boy would take his turn at it, standing astraddle the stone, bending double to pick it up with both hands, and swinging it back and forth between his legs in order to give it as great a heave as possible. As Ted watched, several of the players managed to send the rock several yards; and he suddenly felt a desire to try his hand at it, although he was a good deal bigger than the others.

Something in his face must have told his thoughts, for one of the native boys said something to the others, and immediately all eyes turned to the stranger. Then one spoke slowly and clearly so that Ted might understand.

Although he did not get the whole statement, he understood enough to know that they wanted him to try too, and he smiled and nodded. At this the whole group burst into jabberings of excitement, and made a place for him. Ted stepped to the rock, which was about the size of a small keg of powder, and straddled it as the others had done. With both hands under it, he lifted, surprised at the weight of it.

Now the group of boys was silent and intent. Ted felt their gaze as he swung the stone back and forth a couple of times to get the idea. Then, with a great heave, he sent the rock backwards with all his might. It was a good throw, but the only thing Ted forgot was to let go of the rock.

The laughter of the audience made him blush as he tried to untangle himself from the knot he had twisted into, but he could not help laughing too. He had thrown himself nearly as far as the rock. He felt foolish and awkward, but determined to show that he could be a good sport. He went to the rock, picked it up again, and gave it a long, swinging heave that sent it a good eight feet behind him. Not the record, by any means, but good enough to raise a shout from his new friends.

As the next lads tried, Ted noticed that these savage people had a strong sense of fairness. Each one was trying his hardest to win, yet every one of them cheered as loudly as he could when the others equalled or bettered his own mark.

As he watched the youngsters playing, Ted happened to look up the hill, and saw that the men of the camp were gathering on the open plain above the river bank. He strode quickly up the hill to see what was going on. Four tall young Indians stood in line, facing away from the river; and though the air was still very chilly, they were stripped to loincloths and moccasins. Ted realized that they were going to have a race, and he looked to the far end of the field, where it rose over a hill about a quarter of a mile away. A sudden shout made him look back to the camp, and he saw the crowd of youngsters charging up the hill to join their fathers and brothers.

Silence fell, and the runners gathered themselves for the dash. A sharp command cracked out, making them leap forward, and dust spurted from under their pounding feet as they sped over the dry grassland. Ted found himself staring at them with his mouth open, for these brown athletes ran like the wind. They strode with long, smooth grace, their feet falling on the heel and rolling on the ball, with a flowing of muscles that reminded Ted of the easy bound of an antelope. They reached the top of the slope at the end of the field, and he watched to see them turn and come racing back; but instead they disappeared over the crest of the hill. Ted did not know what to think.

The crowd waited quietly, and some of them made bets with their friends. Expecting to see the runners come dashing back over the hill at any moment, Ted waited for five minutes, ten, and fifteen, until there came a cry from one of the boys. Arms pointed far across the grass, to tiny figures that were rounding a rise of land two miles away. And they disappeared around it, still running strongly, still heading south.

Ted gasped. What kind of race was this? He asked some of the youths how far the race was to go; but though they seemed to understand his crude Blackfoot, all he could make out in their reply was "Spitzee". Spitzee! Why, that was about fifteen miles away. Races were good sport, thought Ted; but running to Spitzee and back, just for fun . . . ! Now he understood why these men had been sent out to chase in the buffalo. Runners like that did not need horses.

Just thinking about it made Ted feel tired; he walked back to the camp and sat down beside the creek. The celebration was still going full strength. The Indians, having worked off the effects of their first meal, came back for more; and so the feast lasted all day and far into the night.

Some time after midday, when the sun had started to slide into the western sky, a party of horsemen rode into the camp. Ted was surprised at this, for no stranger ever got close to the camp without raising an alarm from the lookout. He got up and went over to have a look at the newcomers. There were six, all braves, and some wore elaborate clothes and feathered headdresses. Ted heard the word "Sarcee" mentioned by the people close to him. These, then, were the Sarcees, warlike allies of the Blackfeet, and regarded as part of the Blackfoot Nation. After the first greetings, the crowd thinned and the visitors left their ponies in the care of several Blackfoot men while they entered the tepee of Battle Drum, probably to smoke the pipe.

Ted turned away and walked back to his seat by the creek. Even though it was growing cold, he sat there for some time, watching the swirling water and thinking of how best to make his escape. He was tempted to slip into the creek there and then, and swim quietly downstream until he was far past the camp. But then he would have to leave his rifle and gear behind, and he did not wish to do that. The water would be bitterly cold, too, he thought with a shiver.

At that moment a shadow fell across him and he heard a

soft footstep. Behind him was one of the Sarcees, who spoke in very good English, as Ted got to his feet:

"My friends the Blackfeet have told me of the slayer of the great mountain bear, and I have come to meet him. I myself wear the necklace." And he rattled the dry claws of a necklace similar to Ted's, except that between the claws, instead of wooden beads, there shone the dull yellow gloss of bone.

"Where have you come from?" asked Ted, again seating himself. The Indian sat also, and answered:

"I come from my camp not far to the north and west. From the forests of the hills. We have come on a scouting party and have stopped to pay our respects to our brothers, the Blackfeet." He paused, as though thinking what to say next. "I have been told of your help in the great hunt, and chief Battle Drum wishes me to say that he and his band are very proud to have you in their camp, and very happy to know that your rifle shoots for them instead of at them."

"But if they think that, why do they keep me prisoner in the camp?" Ted asked.

"You are not a prisoner," the Indian told him. "Did you not understand when they asked you to help them? They gave you your freedom many days ago. You may walk out of this camp any time you wish."

Ted felt his heart jump at this news, but before he could say anything, the Sarcee went on: "But I would give you advice, white hunter. Without a horse you are helpless on the plains at this time of the year. Soon the snow will come, and food will be scarce. Better to wait until these Blackfeet have captured more horses, and then they will give you one so that you may go back to your people. It is a long walk to Edmonton through the winter."

"Oh, do you know Edmonton?" asked Ted.

"Yes. Many times I have been there to trade for powder. We of the Sarcees do not take many pelts, but we have meat and horses that buy all the white man's supplies that we need. But of course we must be careful when we go that far north. As we are brothers of the Blackfeet, we are sworn enemies of the Crees, and even the Assiniboines hold us as poor friends."

"I know that the Blackfeet and Crees are enemies, but where did the Sarcees come from?" Ted wanted to know.

"Many years ago," said the Sarcee, "before even our oldest man can remember, we lived far to the north, nearly as far as the summer snow. We belonged to a tribe known as the Sik-Sika. Somehow it split in two, and one half became the Beaver tribe that still lives in the north country, while the other half came farther south and became the Sarcees.

"Both tribes have their own stories as to how this happened. The Beavers say that a young brave was annoyed by his neighbour's dog, and in a fit of rage slew the animal. The dog's master became angry, and in turn slew the dog-killer. Then the dog-killer's family took up the quarrel and killed the neighbour, and in a short time the whole camp was divided into two bands. And so they separated, one band leaving the camp and moving to the south. These people were the band of the dog-killer, and were called by the others 'Sa arsi', which means 'not good'. This is now the word Sarcee as we say it. The other group took the name Beaver.

"But of course there are two sides to every story, and my tribe tells it this way. The Sik-Sika used to move south each winter, and go back north in the summer. On one such trip they had to cross a small lake that was frozen over. Half the tribe crossed in safety, but then one of the young boys noticed a deer's antler sticking up out of the ice. His mother told him to leave it alone, but he would not, and took hold of it to pull it free of the ice.

"Immediately the whole surface of the lake was broken into tiny pieces, and all those who were in the act of crossing were lost. Those who had not yet crossed could go no farther and had to turn back. They became the Beavers. Those who had already crossed could not return, so they travelled on southward until they came to the place where we now live, and they are the Sarcees. And even today it is believed by my people that all those who perished in the lake became water spirits and may be seen sometimes when the season is right."

The Indian stopped, and Ted was afraid to say anything for fear he would not continue. But when the silence lengthened, he spoke up:

"That is certainly very interesting. Which do you think is the nearer story to the truth?" The Indian shook his head slowly.

"I do not know," he said. "There must be some truth in both of them, but I do not know. Nobody knows. It is an old story."

"But do the Sarcees belong to the Blackfoot Nation?" asked Ted.

"No, not exactly. But we call ourselves cousins, for we are a small tribe, and the Blackfeet are mighty. They are the strongest nation on the plains. We of the Sarcees would have been driven away many years ago had we not made peace with the Blackfeet."

"Blackfeet!" Ted laughed. "I never thought of it before,

but it is a funny name for Indians, isn't it? How do you suppose they got to be called that?"

"There is a legend——" began the Sarcee.

"Tell me," begged Ted. And the Sarcee told him:

"Long ago, when the earth was yet young, there lived a great chieftain. This man was head chief of all the tribes in the land, for at that time they were all united into one great nation. This chief ruled his people well for many years, until one day he had a vision, and knew that he had not long to live, for he was growing very old.

"So he called together all his sons, and there were many of them. They came into his lodge and he said to them, 'I have had a vision and have seen myself singing my death song. When I am dead, one of you must take my place. Which one of you will it be?' And he gazed very fondly at his youngest son, for this lad was his favourite.

"At once there came from the sons a great noise of arguing, for each son felt that he should take his father's place. All but one son, that is. The favourite. This youth was different from his brothers. He was gentle while they were fierce and warlike. He was honest and kind, while they were interested only in themselves no matter what they did to others. He was much loved by his friends while the others were feared and hated by some.

"But this boy was much younger and much smaller than his brothers. And everyone in the tribe knew that a chieftain must be strong and brave to lead his people in safety and prosperity. Still, he was the favourite son, and because of this he was hated by his brothers, so that his life was a trial which he bore without complaint. His father knew this, and saw the wildness in his other sons, and knew that this younger man would make the best chief. And so he formed a plan that would cause the younger son to be made chief.

"When the old man saw that the brothers would not decide for themselves in a peaceful manner, he called to them, 'My sons, do not fight among yourselves. Come, let us hold contests and whichever of you is the best man, he shall take my place.'

"Now the chief knew that his youngest son was as swift a runner as the deer, so he declared that the first competition would be a race. All the sons lined up and started running toward the hilltop across the valley, but as soon as they were out of sight, the older sons threw a stick in front of the younger man, who tripped and fell, so that the others won the race. The younger son did not tell what had happened, and the chief was puzzled to find that he did not win.

"And so he declared another event, wrestling, and the brothers paired off and began to wrestle. The winner of each team was matched with another winner, until all but one had been defeated. Now the young man was slight and slim, but he was also very agile, and managed to throw all his opponents, until at the last, one of his brothers took a handful of dirt and threw it into the lad's eyes when the old man could not see. Blinded, the youth was beaten by his brother, and again the old chief was puzzled. But they must try something else. Next they went hunting.

"The young man was a keen hunter, and tireless on the trail. When each brother was given a trail to follow, they started off through the forest, but deep in the woods the older brothers came upon a wounded deer, which they caught and drove across the younger man's trail, so that he was confused and turned back upon himself, and so lost the contest. By now the old chief was aware of what the brothers were doing to their younger brother, and he called them to him again.

" 'I can see that there can be no peace among you,' he said. 'You are strong men, and will make great chiefs, all of you. But you are not good enough to lead my tribe. Therefore I am going to divide the tribe into many sections, and each of you will be chieftain of one section; but the largest and best section of the tribe I will set aside, to be led by your youngest brother.'

"So saying, he called the boy to him, and bade him lift up his right foot. The old man bent to take a partly burned stick from the fire, and with it he blackened the bottom of the lad's moccasin with the charcoal from the stick. When he had thus marked both moccasins, he said: 'This will show all my people that you are chosen to lead the greatest tribe in the land. And your tribe shall forever be known as the Blackfoot Nation.' And so it is known today, for it is the largest and strongest nation in the land."

The Sarcee sat with bowed head for a little while, then added: "Of course, there are other legends. Some believe that the Indians walked across burned prairie and their moccasins became black. But who is to say which story is true?"

Chapter Eleven

"How did you come to be captured by Battle Drum?" asked the Sarcee. "I was coming from the Spitzee River country when I ran across a scouting party," replied Ted. "I got past them and camped in a big stone west of here. That is where they found me, and I could not get away."

"Okotoks!" exclaimed the Sarcee.

"Yes," said Ted. "That's what they called it. It means 'big rock', does it not?"

"Big Rock is a very special place for the Blackfeet." The Sarcee paused for several moments, and Ted waited. He knew that another story was coming.

"I do not know the story," admitted the Indian, "but I know a woman of this camp who does. We shall go to her."

He rose, and Ted did likewise, interested in what might be learned from the woman. They walked into the camp and the Sarcee strode up to a squaw, demanding in his own language:

"Where is the woman called Prairie Grass, who was the last wife of Buffalo Horn?"

The old woman pointed to a tepee nearby and grinned with toothless gums. "She sits alone in her tent. She is waiting to die."

Ted could not understand the conversation, but the Indian told him what the woman had said, and Ted was concerned over the situation.

"Why doesn't someone help her? Why doesn't the Medicine Man try to make her live? Is she ill or just old?"

"She is very old, that one. She is the youngest wife of Buffalo Horn, one of the greatest warriors of the Blackfoot Nation. He was killed by Crees when I was yet a young boy. That is more than thirty winters ago. She is indeed very old; and when our people become old and no longer able to work in the camp, they are left to themselves, to die or to live, whichever they choose. When the camp moves, they stay behind. It is the custom of my people. But think not of such things. This woman has a tale for you; come and listen."

So saying, he pushed open the flap of the tepee and bent low to step inside. Ted followed, and his eyes could hardly pierce the gloom. The tent was stuffy and airless inside, and quite chilly. The woman sat near the centre, close to a tiny fire that snapped and glowed, and by its light Ted was startled to see the wrinkled face of the old woman, so deeply furrowed that her eyes and mouth seemed like cracks. Her bony hands, bare and brown, lay folded on her lap. The Sarcee spoke softly to her, and she answered him in short words, hardly heard in the silence.

"She speaks no English, nor any tongue but Blackfoot," whispered the Indian. "I will tell you what she says." And he seated himself facing the crone. Ted also sat facing her, and immediately they were settled the woman picked up a heavy pipe from near the fire and began to suck on it. Then she spoke.

"The Okotoks is a stone," translated the Sarcee. "It is a high stone, and many winters past a man camped by it. He put a blanket on the stone; but the sky began to rain, and because he did not want his blanket to get wet the man took up his blanket again. When he did so, the rock called out to him: 'No one gives anything to a stone and takes it back'; whereupon it began to roll toward the man.

"The man was very frightened, and ran away. But the stone rolled swiftly after him. The man ran as fast as he could, but the stone was almost upon him when a deer passed by. 'Help, help! Save me!' cried the man; but the stone rolled over the deer and killed it, and kept on rolling after the man. Soon they met a bear, and the man called out 'Help, help! Save me!' But the stone rolled right over the bear and killed it.

"And the stone kept rolling after the man, and had almost caught up to him when they came to a flock of birds. 'Help, help! Save me!' cried the terrified man, and the flock of birds took to the air and swooped down upon the rolling rock. Again and yet again they attacked, and the rock trembled and began to slow. The fourth time the birds swooped, the rock cracked into two pieces and stopped, and the man was saved, and the rock lay where it stopped; and that is where it is today. That is the story of the okotoks."

"Is there anything else you would like to know about the

rock?" asked the Sarcee when the old woman had finished. "You may not find another who has known so much about the old days."

"Yes, I would like to ask another question." Ted did not want to go away without finding out all he could about this part of the country. "Ask her if the crossing of this river is named for the big stone."

The question was translated to the old woman, and in a moment she gave her answer.

"The crossing is known as 'the crossing of the river by the big stone', and is sometimes called Stone Crossing, and the river is called Stone River."

Ted caught the word 'Okotokseeka', and learned that it meant Stony River, or Stone River. Then he noticed that the old woman appeared to be very tired, for her eyes kept closing and her head nodded. He looked at the man, and they rose, thanking the woman, and went out into the fresh air.

"I would have liked to ask her about the pictures on the stone," said Ted, as they walked away. "Can you tell me anything about them?"

"I have seen them," replied the Indian, "but I can tell you nothing of them. They were put there many years before my family came to this part of the country. It is believed that they were put there by ancient gods, and none who are left can read them."

"Oh, that's too bad." Ted was really sorry, for he felt that the signs would tell much. He thanked the Sarcee for his kindness and said goodbye.

Noticing a crowd of boys in a corner of the camp, Ted walked over to see what was going on. They were formed in a circle about two half-naked youths, who stood facing each other with their right hands firmly clasped and their feet placed on a straight line. Each was straining to make the other lose balance, so that his feet would move from the line. The crowd yelled encouragement as the wrestlers struggled first one way and then another, until one of them, with a sudden backward movement, pulled his opponent off balance and the match was over. Immediately another pair took their places on the line, and were in turn cheered by the crowd.

This was good sport, but Ted did not feel like trying his hand at it, after the fool he had made of himself earlier in the day. He watched for a while as the boys jerked and pushed and pulled at each other, hands clasped tightly, arms hard with straining muscles. Something about the arms and hands made him look closer. They were pitted and streaked with white marks, and Ted realized that these marks were scars. And then he noticed that the arms and the bodies of nearly all those around him were covered with tiny white scars. Now he had another mystery to solve. He looked around, trying to spot his Sarcee friend.

The Indian was some distance away, talking with some other braves. Ted walked over and waited until the talk was finished. Then the Sarcee turned to him and asked:

"What does my white friend want to know?"

Ted told him about the scars he had seen. "What do they do to make those marks?"

"They do that when they are learning to be brave," answered the Indian. "Watch for a while. You will see them doing it." And so saying, he went away, leaving Ted still wondering. But he did not have to wonder very much longer.

The wrestling gradually slowed and stopped, and then

several older lads began to argue among themselves, and in a moment the whole band moved toward one side of the camp. Ted followed, and they stopped under a small spruce tree that stood near the water. One of the boys reached up and stripped a low bough from the tree, and each boy in the group plucked one twig from it.

Then Ted saw how the boys came by their marks. As he watched, four of them stood in a circle, and each picked a needle from the twig he held. The needles were placed on the backs of the boys' hands, and a burning ember was touched to them. They flared up hotly, searing the flesh, and Ted saw that the pain was hardly felt by the boys.

He realized that they had been doing this most of their lives, burning themselves on hands and bodies, learning to withstand pain. The smell of scorched skin drifted past him, and he saw that some of the braver boys were pressing live coals to each other's chests. For half an hour they played thus, growing more daring with each new challenge. Then this game too became dull, and they wandered away to find something else to do.

Ted sat again by the stream, listening and watching, until nearly sundown. And just before the sun went down he caught a sudden murmur of excitement from the elders. Coming over the hill was a runner, one of those who had left the camp some hours before.

Ted did some rapid figuring and was rather puzzled. The runners were to go to Spitzee, which was perhaps fifteen miles, or less. This man had taken about six hours to make it there and back. That would come to about five miles an hour. A pony walking could do that, and these men ran much faster than a walking horse.

What had delayed them? Had they rested part of the

time? Ted did not think so. He knew that once an Indian sets his mind to a task, he does not stop until it is done. He did not find out until many days later that while the runners had gone to Spitzee, they had done so only after running some twenty miles east to a height of land, and then back to the river at Spitzee, making a total course of nearly sixty miles.

The first runner to come into camp was quickly surrounded by his friends, and much laughing and whooping showed that he was the hero of the day. Half an hour later the rest of the runners loped into view, still running easily and strongly, still running for the thrill of the sport, and not caring too much that they had not won.

Ted turned to his tepee and lay sleepless, listening to the sounds from around the fires. He was glad that the natives did not have any whiskey, or there would be much more to worry about than trying to sleep. As he listened the wind dropped its voice a bit, and the sounds of revelry came clearer, but another sound took Ted's attention. It was the sound of breathing. Not the breathing of humans, but more like the snuffle of a horse.

A horse! Ted rose as quietly as he was able, and crept to the flap. Somewhere close to him was a horse. And in a moment he heard it again. Not only one, but a number of horses were close by. He cautiously pushed aside the flap and peered out; and presently, under the large willows, he saw the darker shadow of a horse and rider. From behind the tent came other sounds, the rustle of leather leggings against horsehide, the scrape of hooves on dead wood.

Ted's first impulse was to make a dash for it and warn the Blackfeet; but he quickly realized that it was too late.

The raiders would overtake him in a moment, and he would lose his life for his pains.

Very slowly he closed the flap and sank to the ground, so that he would not cast a shadow on the tent wall should the firelight shine through. The sounds moved past the tent, and he knew that the raiders trusted that all the camp was taking part in the celebration. Quietly he moved back until he reached the rear of the tepee, and there he felt with his hand for one of the rocks that held down the cover. With both hands he shoved it back, then he lifted the bottom of the tepee and crawled out, every movement slow and careful.

Suddenly the whole valley seemed to explode. The thunder of charging horses was drowned out by the war cries of the attackers; then the screams of terror from the Blackfeet women welled up above all other sounds.

Ted darted like a rabbit into the underbrush and sped through the dark aisles of willows, while the sounds grew fainter behind him; then a sickening realization burst upon his mind and he stopped dead. He had forgotten his rifle and hunting pouch!

For a moment he stood in indecision; then he turned and ran back. He was risking his life; but to be weaponless in the hills in winter would very likely mean his death anyway.

Coming near the camp again, Ted slowed down and approached with caution. The noise of the short-lived battle had died away, and he could hear the voices and see the dim shapes of the marauders as they moved among the tents, searching them. At the moment there was no one near his own tepee, and dropping to the ground he crawled silently to the back of it and lay there, listening intently. No sound came from within, so he raised the cover and slipped inside.

Quickly Ted located his hunting pouch, lying where he had left it against the wall of the tepee; but his rifle was not in its usual place. Frantically but without noise, he searched the tent. Yes, there was no doubt of it; the raiders had already been there, and his rifle was gone!

Sick at heart, he crawled back to the forest again, a shadow against the ground. Once within the protection of the trees, he rose to his feet and moved carefully ahead until a safe distance separated him from the camp; then he broke into a trot and made his way to the river, where he travelled upstream.

Chapter Twelve

FROM a distance Ted looked back at the Blackfoot camp. The raiders had set fire to it, and the bright flames of the burning tents lit up the bare banks of the river. For a short time he watched, then he turned and pursued his way upstream.

Through his mind there passed the memory of the time he had fled up the Spitzee River like this, leaving behind his father's burning cabin; and his thoughts turned to the friendly hills that had sheltered him then. There, to the west, was a country he knew. Even though it was many miles from his old cave, it was the same kind of country, and he knew that there he could make his home for the winter.

As he walked along the edge of the river, the chill night air began to bite through his clothes. He thought how lucky he was that his captors had allowed him to keep the warm clothing he had brought from Edmonton. But even though he began to grow cold, he could not stop to warm himself. He must put many more miles between the Indians and himself.

He stumbled on over the rough gravel until he felt it was safe to stop; then he found a big rock to sit on, and by the light of the stars he counted his assets. The belt held his knife and powder horn, shot bag and cap box. His pouch contained the pistol, some dried slivers of meat and his flint.

Sight of the flint suddenly seemed to make the wind feel colder, and he began to shiver as he gathered dry bark and twigs. The bark he shredded until it was like a ball of hair, and the twigs he snapped from standing live trees, so that he was sure the wood was dry, and not soaked from touching the damp ground. With numb fingers he struck the flint against his knife, making bright sparks in the darkness, and in another five minutes his little fire was snapping happily under the shelter of the bank.

He crouched close but could not drive out the chill that had settled over him. If he warmed his hands and chest, his back grew cold, and if he turned himself around to warm his back, he grew cold in the front. And then he remembered the Indian trick. What was it the Indians used to say —something about "white man build big fire and freeze; Indian build small fire and keep warm." Yes, that was it. So he searched along the bank for a log of the right size. He found it a little farther along the bank, and built up a small pile of wood under one side. Then he took a handful of bark and used it to carry his flame to the new place.

Seating himself directly over the fire, with the blaze flickering between his feet, he felt the warmth of the flames slowly creeping up his legs. The Indians sat this way, and draped a blanket across their shoulders to the ground, making the heat rise up all around them. Ted had no blanket to hold in the heat, but even so the smoke that rose around him was warmer than the night air, and he managed to keep fairly comfortable; and the fuel needed to feed the fire was as close as the log on which he sat.

Hunched double over the fire, arms resting on his thighs, Ted found himself dozing; and before long the sky began to brighten. When he could see the far side of the creek, he stirred up the coals and piled more wood on the fire. While the flames licked up the sticks, he went to the river and splashed himself with the icy water. Feeling refreshed and ready to meet the coming day, he looked around for something to eat. Once again he was left to rely on his own resources, and he wished mightily for his old rifle. Well, it was no use moaning about it. He would have to use what he had.

Of course he did have the pistol and powder, but he did not want to use it unless he had to. He wandered a short way up the river, looking for signs of rabbits or grouse, and it was not long before he caught sight of a white form. The rabbit had already put on its winter coat, which made it easy for Ted to spot in the brush and brown dry grass. He stalked it as he had learned so many years before. The rabbit hopped innocently along the bank, and Ted moved in very slowly. He froze in his tracks as the little animal moved a few steps toward him. He did not move, and the rabbit hopped closer, nibbling fussily at every piece of grass that caught its fancy.

Ted could hardly keep from laughing as he watched its pink nose wiggling; and then the rabbit took another hop that brought it within a few feet of the waiting boy. For several minutes the two sat close to each other, the rabbit eating, the boy wondering if he dared try to grab it. So still did they sit that the hawk high above them saw only the white form of the rabbit.

The first hint Ted had of the coming action was a shrill whistle. He did not know what to make of it, but the rabbit did. It hunched as close to the ground as it was able, knowing that the slightest move it made would be sure death. Ted did not even have time to look up to see what was making the noise before the bird struck. The rabbit gave a shrill shriek of fright as it leaped in a desperate effort to evade the falling doom. It jumped right into Ted's lap, and he grabbed it with both hands and ducked, all automatically.

The hawk, swooping to clutch its escaping prey, screamed in surprise and stopped a foot from the ground. Its wings beat the air frantically in an effort to avoid the monster that loomed up before it, and there came a crack like a rifle shot from the shock of the sudden stop. Then the hawk flapped up and soared away, screaming its opinion of meal-thieves.

Ted sat for a moment holding the rabbit tightly, breathing hard to catch his breath, and the rabbit lay still as death save for the furious pounding of its heart and the quivering of its body. Ted felt sorry for the poor creature; but still, he had to live too. He held the bunny by its ears and with the edge of his hand struck it a sharp blow at the base of the skull. The rabbit kicked violently and the quivering slowly lessened. He took it back to the fire and skinned it out. The pelt he rolled and tied to his pouch, and the carcass he cleaned and cooked.

It did not take long to broil over his hot little fire, and it took even less time for him to eat it. Ted picked the bones clean before he finished. He put out the fire, spread sand over the traces of burned wood, and erased all footprints he could see around. Then he took up his pouch and started up the river again. This river of the Okotoks was not as wide as the Spitzee, nor so rock-bound, most of the way, but it ran swiftly between high banks, and the bush grew only in a few places this far out on the plains. Unlike the Spitzee stream, trees did not follow along the river all the way down. There was poor protection from the wind, and from sight by enemy eyes.

The hills, though, seemed closer here, and by the end of the day Ted was nearing the foothills. He made his camp in a small cave in the river bank and another rabbit became his supper. Before the sun went down, he had time to walk through a little patch of woods close by, and in a low, damp, shadowed part he found a number of soft white plants that the Indians had taught him to pick—or *were* these the ones? He remembered that some similar plants were poisonous, and he sat for a little while trying to recall which were which. Finally he decided that these were safe to eat, and he picked a double handful of them.

They were dry and withered, but they were food, so he toasted them over his fire and tasted them. They were not as fresh as they might have been, or as tender, but he found that they had a strange earthy flavour that he had enjoyed in the Blackfoot camp, so he ate all that he had picked. He ate most of the rabbit too.

Feeling much better for a full stomach, he turned to his shelter, and found that by building his fire near the opening, he could keep it fairly warm. He curled up close to the heat, rolling over each time he became cold on one side.

He slept that night, and dreamed of a warm, dry dugout in the hills, with a blazing fireplace and shelves full of flour and tea and salt, and a grease lamp flickering against the ceiling.

The following day was cold and sunless, and Ted moved quickly to keep warm. He ate a few scraps of the rabbit that were left over, and was soon on the trail upstream again. This time he travelled on the bench above the stream, for here it was possible to see for miles. The hills grew higher and higher, and he strained his eyes for the sight of the first mountain. By climbing a small hill he saw it; and to his surprise, it was not far away. The sight of it made his blood leap, and he ran happily down the hill.

It was soon after this that he came to a beaver pond. At first sight of the intruder the nearest beaver brought down his great flat tail on the water, and the sound cracked like a shot. Others did the same, then all was still as the animals dived under the surface and disappeared.

Here was food and fur. Ted remembered the beaver he had trapped in the mountains, and he remembered how delicious was the meat. There were a lot of beaver in this pond, but he had no trap, no rifle, no snare, not even a spear. But he could make a beaver spear. He went to the nearest tree, a large bushy willow, and cut a long heavy pole, as thick as his wrist at the butt end, tapering smoothly to a sharp point, and about twelve feet long. He built a small fire and heated the sharpened small end in the flame, almost burning the wood, making the point hard and sharp. He had his spear.

He waded to the nearest beaver lodge and climbed up onto it. It lay low in the water, like a mud island, and all around were the criss-crossed piles of green cuttings that the busy animals were storing up for their winter supply of food. Looking closely into the water immediately around the house he stood on, Ted soon discovered the muddy trail where the beaver had entered. He put the end of his spear into the water just above this track and lowered it slowly until the point struck the mud bottom. Then he pulled it a little upwards, perhaps six or seven inches. He braced himself, gripped the pole firmly with both hands, one at the end of the stick, and waited.

He waited for five minutes—ten minutes—he did not know how long, but the muscles of his legs cried out with pain under the strain of his crouch. Then, across the pond, a brown head broke the quiet surface, and the hump of the back rose out of the water, making two tiny islets in the pond. Little wavelets drifted idly away from the disturbance, making rings that lapped one after another against the sticks of the houses. Another beaver surfaced, and the pair lay still in the water as they watched and waited for any sign of danger; then they swam strongly to the place where they had been interrupted at their labours.

One after another the inhabitants of the village began to return to work, and Ted wondered if he had made a mistake. But he pushed the tip of his spear downward ever so slightly, and kept still. In a moment he felt the pole quiver as the beaver swam out and scraped against it. As quickly and strongly as he could, he thrust down his spear. He felt the point drive through flesh and bone, and the end of the pole was nearly wrenched from his grasp; but he pushed harder and harder until it would go no farther down. The pole jerked and heaved like a living thing as the beaver struggled, and the water around the entrance to the lodge became tinted pink.

Slowly the struggle ceased. When he was sure it was all over, Ted withdrew the spear; and in a moment the body, borne up by countless bubbles of air in the fur, bobbed up close to him. With the spear he pulled it to him; and it took a good grip with both hands on the paddle-tail to lift it out of the water. It was a large buck, and would provide him with several good meals. He cradled it in his arms and, dragging the spear, waded back to shore.

In his life with the Indians, Ted had learned the reason for their great liking for beaver tail; it was perhaps the most delicious meat he had ever eaten. So now he skinned his beaver, roasted a portion of the tail, and ate his fill. Then he dressed the carcass and lashed it by the legs to his crude spear with strips cut from the animal's hide. The skin he rolled with the others and tied them to his pouch again; then, with the spear over his shoulder, he went on his way.

The third day of travel brought him into the mountains. He stopped at the great rock wall and looked up to the heights. In the long grey line of peaks, there was only this one valley in sight that would let him pass through. He walked along the creek floor, past great hills and through deep canyons. One huge slab of stone reared high above him, leaning out threateningly over the valley; and he found himself eyeing it nervously as he hurried past.

Once past the hanging cliff, he was well into the mountains and began to feel almost at home. The first thing he must do was find shelter, some place where he could stay all winter. His camp that night was in the valley, for the woods rose all around and there was no trail through them save the flatland along the creek. He cooked the rest of his beaver meat and slept under the roots of a great wind-felled tree.

The rattle of antlers against wood awoke Ted. It was early dawn and as yet it was too dark to see much in the shadows of the trees. Slowly and carefully he reached for his rifle, before he remembered it was not there. His hand felt for the hunting pouch, and drew out the pistol. Holding it ready, he stuck his head out of the shelter under the tree and looked around. Again the sound came, and he could just make out a figure moving in the gloom. For a long while he held his place, gun pointed but not cocked. The noise of the hammer cocking would carry a long way on such a still morning, and probably frighten the beast. He dared not chance a shot in the half-light. Every ball was precious and every loud sound would frighten away other game.

Slowly the grey shadows lifted. The animal stayed where it was, and little by little Ted was able to see it more clearly. It was an elk, and not twenty yards away. It was a long shot with a pistol; how he wished for his rifle! He raised the gun very slowly and took aim, using both hands to steady it, and his thumb drew back the hammer. It clicked sharply on the still air, and the elk raised its head, staring wildly toward the boy but not seeing any hostile movement. It stood thus for a few moments, while Ted lined his sights; then the gun roared and bucked in his hands. A cloud of smoke billowed around the woods, hiding target and all, but Ted stayed where he was until it cleared, waiting to see the result of his shot.

The elk was dead, and Ted knew that he had a big job ahead of him that morning. He cleaned the pistol and re-loaded the empty chamber. Then he set to work to skin and cut up the carcass. Here was a supply of meat that would last him many days, but it had to be cured before it spoiled; so he built a good fire, letting it burn down to coals while he cut the meat into long, thin strips. These strips he hung on long poles above the fire, where they would not cook but simply dry to hard slivers. In this condition they would last for a long time without going bad.

He camped in the valley for two days, grudging the time, but knowing that he was wise in doing so. When he had finished with the elk, he had dried nearly a hundred pounds of meat and scraped clean a large hide. His belongings were now quite bulky and he rolled the meat and other skins into one bundle inside the elk hide, making up a large pack that weighed nearly a hundred and fifty pounds. His first attempt to lift it to his back showed him that he could not carry such a load, so he was forced to unpack it and leave out half the meat. This made a pack that he could easily shoulder, and he slung it across his back, picked up his pouch and spear, and started again along the valley floor.

He had not gone two miles when he jumped the second animal. This time it was a large deer, and his hasty shot only staggered it. Before he could drop his pack and leap upon it with his knife, it jumped to its feet and bounded away up the hill toward the south. Ted ran to where the deer had been hit, and from the splashes of blood on the grass he knew that it could not go far. His frugal mind could not let this chance go to waste, especially when he needed the hide so badly, so he turned after the wounded creature.

Within a few yards of the creek he found the trail. It was a well-used animal trail, leading far to the south, up over the hills and through the thickest part of the forests. For several miles Ted followed the track before he realized that it was leading him up to a pass of some kind between the great peak on his right and the grey rock wall on his left. He was surprised that the deer could travel so far and so fast, for it was bleeding a great deal, to judge by the continuous red line along the path.

Ted pressed on up the hill as fast as he was able, but the pack on his back made climbing hard. The trail grew steeper and steeper, until he found himself on a long saddle between the two mountain peaks; and as he stopped to catch his breath he gazed up the great tower of stone on the right, toward the peak that was hidden in the clouds. From where he rested, Ted could look down into a valley to the south; and he could look far out across the miles and miles of hills and valleys, right across the whole countryside, to the next range of mountains.

When he had rested and regained his breath, Ted started on the trail again; but now the path led downward into the valley. Where the stunted trees began he found the deer, dead.

He set to work to skin the animal, then took a few choice parts, such as the tongue and liver. On a little level place nearby he built a fire and set up camp for the night. While he cooked the fresh meat, he looked around the hills. He was a thousand feet below the ridge over which he had entered this valley, but even so he was still high above the surrounding countryside.

He sat on the hillside and ate his meal, looking out over the dim distance. Somewhere far down that valley, he told himself, was his old dugout. His heart leaped at the thought and he felt a pang of homesickness; but then he realized that he did not know how far it was. It might be fifty miles, for all he could tell.

He let his eyes wander up and down the wild hillsides; and then suddenly, a little way down the very hill on which he sat, he saw a thin plume of smoke.

Smoke! Whose was it—white or Indian, friend or enemy? He felt a thrill go through him, partly of joy, partly of fear; and for five minutes he sat very still, trying to make up his mind. Should he turn back the way he had come, or go boldly into the other camp? He decided to do neither. He would scout this camp and find out who was there.

With his mind made up, he cached all his meat and hides in a rocky crevice, covering it with stones to keep animals out; and taking his pistol, he began the descent to the place whence the smoke came. It took him over an hour to get there, pausing often, eyes watching for signs of movement, ears alert for any sound.

Beyond a ridge just ahead of him the smoke was rising, but still he could hear nothing. He crawled carefully and silently to the top of the ridge and peered over. At first he saw nothing but the windswept rocks and the stunted trees; but then, as he watched, a wreath of smoke drifted upward; seeming to come from a gulley just in front of him; and then to his listening ears came a queer hissing noise. Not exactly hissing, though; rather like bubbling, like a great pot boiling. They must be cooking up a big meal, thought Ted to himself, and stayed where he lay for a while longer.

With each passing minute he became aware of something he did not understand. The smoke from the campfire rolled up and drifted down the hillside, but when he sniffed, there came no smell of burning wood. And still he had not seen any sign of movement, either human or animal. Ted grew tired of waiting, and became impatient. He raised himself to his feet and, with his gun ready, stepped silently over the rocks until he stood directly above the camp. A sudden gust of wind caught at the pall of smoke, and whipped it upward to envelop him. He gasped, choked on the heavy odour of sulphur, and ducked out of the cloud, frightened. When he had stopped coughing, he scrambled to the edge of the gulley and looked down.

The gurgling and bubbling noise was loud now, and before his eyes Ted saw the source of the stinking vapour. From a crack in the solid rock wall of the cleft flowed a blue stream of boiling-hot water. The reek of sulphur filled the air, and Ted found that he gradually became used to it. He sat on the edge of the ravine and looked at the hot spring, fascinated by the sight of the water as it bubbled and gushed forth in a steady flow, and the vapour turned to steam in the chill mountain air, looking for all the world like smoke.

Ted looked around him again, and saw the tall mountain leaning back into the sky. He saw the green forests and the shining ribbons of streams on all sides. He saw also the blanket of new snow on the hill tops, and knew that winter was at hand. He could go no farther without running the danger of being caught in the first blizzard. Here was shelter, food, water and everything else he might need before spring. Here he would build his camp.

Chapter Thirteen

TED slept on the mountain grass that night, and if it had not been for the skins he would have been very cold. As it was, the green hides offered only a little warmth, but they did protect him somewhat from the freezing wind that blew off the snowbanks all around. He made his bed by spreading one of the hides on the rocks with the hair side up, and the other on top of it with the hair side down, so that they made a comparatively cosy nest for him to crawl into. He tucked them close about him and finally fell asleep.

When he woke next morning, he could hardly move. It was not that he was stiff, but the hides were. The green skins had partly dried and partly frozen, and he could barely crawl from between them. The sun was shining, and the sulphur spring was running as happily as on the night before, its steam making clouds that lay in the little gulley until they lazily overflowed, to drift down the hillside.

For his breakfast Ted cooked some more of the meat of the deer, washing it down with cold water from another spring, for the hot water was not good to drink. Then the two hides claimed his attention, and he found a level place on the hillside where he stretched them out, skin side up, holding down the corners with rocks, so that the sun would dry them properly before he cured them. Then he looked for a shelter for the winter.

He did not have to look far, for the whole gulley above the hot spring was pitted with caves, some very small, some quite large. He chose one that was big enough to make a fair-sized room, and had a wide ledge in front of it. He spent half an hour inspecting it from all angles, deciding what could most easily be done to turn it into a weather-proof home for the winter. It seemed to be in a good location, far enough up the bank of the gulley so that melting snows would not drown him out, far enough from the hot spring to escape the sulphur fumes, and close enough to the tree line to assure him a plentiful supply of game and firewood.

His next concern was to dry a good supply of meat from the carcass of the deer, storing it in a nearby hole, the mouth of which he blocked with stones to keep out marauding animals. Then he began the work of getting his winter quarters ready.

He started to build a wall of stones and mud across the mouth of the cave. At one side he planned to leave a small space for a doorway, which would be covered with a piece of hide. The wall was a laborious job, and before it was finished he felt the need to do something else to relieve the monotony.

He thought of going after more hides, but this raised

another problem—how was he going to kill large animals, such as deer and elk, if he did find any? He had only the pistol, and there were precious few caps for it. All the powder and ball in the country would be of no use without caps, and those he had must be saved for an emergency.

No, the pistol could not be used for everyday hunting. He must find another way, something that would serve again and again, and would not require powder and lead. He sat by the cave, thinking; and when he finally arrived at the answer to his problem, he was surprised that he had not thought of it long before, when he had first left the Blackfoot camp at Okotoks crossing. How, he wondered, could he possibly have forgotten the bow—the faithful Indian bow and arrows? He remembered when he had seen his Stony friends sink arrows feather-deep in the sides of buffalo. He had seen them bring down deer at a hundred paces.

The bow, he knew, was one of the oldest weapons on the plains, and if the Indians could survive for hundreds of years with it, surely he could get through the winter. Then he was sorry he had not made one while out on the banks of the river. The Indians usually chose the wood of the service tree for their bows. There were great clumps of these bushes along the river he had left a few days before, but certainly none this high up on the mountain. He would have to go back to the river if he was to get the proper wood.

Meanwhile, all he had to use was the long spear he had brought with him. He picked it up and looked at it. The stick was about ten feet long, for he had broken it several times and whittled new points on it. The butt end was about half the thickness of his wrist. It was a willow stave, still green and supple. As a spear, it would not be of much use for large animals; but cut down into a bow, it would serve until something better showed itself.

So his spear became his bow. He spent the rest of the day on this job. First he cut the spear in half. Then he peeled the bark and trimmed off the knots. As half the stave was about the right size for one end, he had only to shave the thicker end down to match, and within a short while he held a rather clumsy, but very springy, bow. Notches at the ends would hold the string. Of course, he would have to wait until the green wood dried so that it was strong and hardened. He laid it across two flat stones and weighed the centre down with another so that it would dry with a slight bend.

By the time this was finished it was nearly dark, and he built up his little fire for cooking. Unable to do more that day, he lay inside his cave, thinking of what still had to be done. There was a chimney to build, and the fireplace, and the bow to make, and hunting to do, for he needed skins and meat; and when the meat was killed, there was the drying of some, and the snow pits for the rest, and the curing of the hides, and making clothing, and—oh, there was so much yet to be done that he fell asleep thinking about it.

In the morning he went back to working on the wall across the cave mouth. Against this would be his fireplace, so a part of the wall was curved out to serve as a chimney. The fireplace itself consisted of an enclosure within two sides, each about a foot high by a foot and a half long.

Ted's next job was building a smokehouse so that he could partially cure his hides. He found a place where the cliff face jutted out in an overhang, and there he leaned a number of logs against the cliff to form a rough enclosure. Inside he hung the hides, and then built a fire of green wood that filled the place with a heavy smoke. He could not cure the hides completely, for this required a mash made from animals' brains and livers; but smoking them would be better than nothing.

Now he examined the bow, and found that it had dried into a good curve. All he needed was the string; and he wished that he had thought to take the large sinew from the dead elk, for it would have made the best string. Then he remembered the deer that had led him to this place, and in a moment he was climbing up the slope to where its remains lay. But to his bitter disappointment, the coyotes had been there before him, and all that remained was a few well-gnawed bones. Ted was stumped. He had a bow, but where was he to get a string? A thin thong from one of the hides might serve; but then leather was soft and would stretch, and that would be no good at all.

The Indians often used bark for strings and thongs. If only he had some long strips of willow bark—what about the spear? He had shredded the bark of the bow stave, but there was still the other half of the spear. Perhaps it was not yet too dry. He ran down the hill to his cave and took out the stick. It was getting pretty dry to peel easily, but perhaps if he put it in water for a while——

A few hours of soaking made the bark almost as green as if alive again, and it peeled from the stick in long slippery strips. Of course, it was not the rough outer bark he wanted, but the soft, pliable inner bark that was nearly as strong as sinew when it was green. He used all care possible as he stripped off the bark and separated the strands, and in a little while he had several long strings of the yellow fibre. These he laid together and twisted and rolled into one long, hard string, and when it was measured to the proper length and loops tied in the ends, it slipped nicely into the notches in the ends of the bow stave. It was just long enough to make the bow bend in a graceful arc, and when Ted plucked the string it twanged musically. He held the bow and drew back the string to test its strength, and the bow bent evenly. Though it was not as stiff as he had hoped, Ted knew that as it dried it would get stronger. No matter, the bow was ready. Now he could go hunting.

He took the bow in his hand, grabbed his hunting bag and stepped toward the edge of his rocky ledge, ready to hit the trail. But before he got more than a few feet from his cave he realized that something was wrong. Something was missing. All of a sudden he knew what it was, and felt very, very foolish. He had no arrows! He had to make some kind of arrows quickly, until he had more time to make them properly. Good arrows need feathers and heavy points to make them fly true, but Ted knew that would have to wait, and decided on straight sticks for his arrow shafts.

He walked down the stream to where the first green bushes were growing and selected several of the straightest shoots. He cut them close to the ground so as to get the longest possible, and took them back to his cave. Immediately he set to work shaving off the bark, trimming off all bumps and knots, and whittling points and notches at opposite ends.

His hunting would still have to wait, for the sticks were very green and heavy, and he knew they would be nearly useless for arrows as they were. He placed them under flat rocks to hold them straight while they dried, and turned resignedly to other things. Finally the day came when he felt that his bow and arrows were ready for the first trial hunt.

The hot spring was plain to see that morning, for the air was frosty at such a height, and the warm water made a little trail of steam all the way down. He followed it into a larger creek far down on the valley floor, and looking back up the mountain, he could almost pick out his cave by its closeness to the steaming spring.

Now he had to find game, for the winter would soon be upon him. There could not be more than a few weeks more of the fine weather, at most, and Ted had little put away for either food or clothing. He stood very still in the valley, listening and waiting.

Chapter Fourteen

FOR several minutes there was no sound in the valley save that of the breeze, and the first slight rustle of life came from close beside Ted. He turned his head slowly, to see a grouse picking seeds from a low bush. Raising his bow, he notched an arrow and took aim at his first target. At the twang of the string the bird jumped, and the shaft wobbled through the air to land two feet from where it was supposed to. Ted took his time. He knew that this grouse would not fly far, and he could practise on it all day if he wished. But he was too far from it for accurate shooting with his crude bow.

He notched another arrow and crept toward the bird. It had perched on a low limb of a pine tree, grey-blue feathers making a good target against the dusty green. Ted drew the string more carefully this time, and farther back than before. He felt each inch of the wood strain, and waited for the snap. But it held, and when the string touched his cheek he held for a moment, centred the point and released the shaft. This time it flew more swiftly, and more accurately too, for it struck the bird squarely, piercing the wing feathers and knocking the grouse to the ground. Ted leaped upon it and wrung its neck before it could utter a squawk.

He held it up and looked at it with pride, for it was his first kill with the new bow. Then he pulled out his arrow and stuffed the bird into his pouch. The first arrow lay nearby, and he picked it up, not wanting to use it again, but not wanting to waste it either. It might come in handy for some emergency. He was happy then. He had the power to hunt. Better still, he had feathers to make better arrows.

But one grouse would not last a hungry lad long. He began to move slowly along the valley floor, making a wide circle of the area, for he did not want to stray too far from his shelter yet. The country was too strange, and there was a chance of getting lost.

Before he had gone thirty feet a small brown body darted across his path and raced into a treetop. From its perch in the high branches of the pine the squirrel chattered and squeaked at Ted, until a whizzing shaft sent it scurrying for shelter. The arrow missed, but at least the young archer was coming closer to his targets by this time. With a little more practice he might do very well with bow and arrows. He wandered on down the valley, searching for easy marks, and before the day was over he had picked off two more grouse as well as several squirrels. At this rate it would not take long to make the new robe he planned. The squirrel robes he had made at the other camp had served him so well that he could think of nothing better to protect him during the coming winter months.

The meat of grouse and squirrels would not carry him through the winter, though, and he began to think of larger game, of the need for meat and hides, and a place to keep the meat so it would not spoil. He thought again of his first hut in the mountains, and of the deep pits he had made, filled with snow and covered with rocks so that the meat inside kept for months without going bad. He would have to make something like that here, he decided. Meanwhile, he plucked the birds and skinned the squirrels. The pelts would go into his robe, the feathers would go onto his arrow shafts, to send them straight and true.

Then he prepared his evening meal. Eating took far less time than the cooking, and in a short while there was little to tell what the birds had looked like, although he saved the squirrel meat for breakfast. There was not much of it, but it would have to do. He wished that he had some flour and vegetables to eat with the meat, for he had found out that a man cannot live well on meat alone.

Ted made a mental note to look for some of the bulbs and roots he had helped the squaws gather in the Blackfoot camp. They would make his food supplies last much longer. There was one plant in particular that he had enjoyed, and he hoped to find some close by, for it grew near water, and there was plenty of water farther down the mountain. He made plans to go root hunting the next day, and then set to work before his fire, peeling more straight sticks for arrows. By cutting thin strips of green hide he managed to bind feathers on to several of the best arrow shafts. The points had become blunt and broken, so he sharpened them and hardened them in the fire.

The next morning was cold and some patches of grass were coated white. Ted was glad he had good moccasins and leggings. After eating the squirrels, he took his bow and the new arrows, slung his hunting pouch over his shoulder, and set out down the mountain side toward the lower end of the valley. He would have to gather all the roots he could find during the next few days, for the late summer was closing and in a short while all plants would be dead, and it would be very hard to recognize the different kinds after the stalks withered away.

The plants he was looking for were the long, hollow-stemmed kind that grew in damp places, and he headed for the nearest meadow, hoping there might be a marshy place in it. When he reached the clearing, there was no sign of water, but in the centre of the area he saw a large patch of the plants. Even then they were beginning to dry up and turn brown, and they snapped and crackled when he grasped the stems. But the stems were not what he was after. The roots were still green and fresh, and the fat round bulbs, like pale green balls, peeled in layers of juicy pulp when broken open. Ted pulled and dug as many as his pouch would hold, and when it was full he turned to digging them up whole, stem and all, and tying the tops together in bunches. He cleaned out the whole patch before stopping; then, well satisfied with his work, he piled his harvest in a heap to await his return from hunting.

The bow had dried more with the passing days, and by this time was getting quite stiff and hard. He kept it strung and held it in readiness, arrow notched, as he stalked into the trees. The first grouse that called was pierced by his first arrow, and he thrilled at the difference the feathers made. Too, he was pleased with the silence of the bow. With a firearm the first shot would have frightened away all the game in the country, but with the bow he could move very quietly through the woods, shooting when and where he liked, without startling anything a hundred yards away.

It was while he was drawing an arrow from a rabbit that he caught sight of the elk. There was not one, but an even dozen of the animals—a bull with his harem of wives. Ted sank to the ground, almost disappearing into the undergrowth. He drew another arrow from his bundle and notched it to the string. The elk were moving slowly up the valley toward the little meadow where he had left the roots. They would pass directly in front of him; Ted would be able to pick off his choice of the whole band before they took fright. He chose the last straggler of the group. If he missed, he would not be seen, and if he struck home, then only one animal would be affected, and there was a chance that the others would not even notice, and he would get a second opportunity.

He crouched lower and breathed lightly as they moved past him, not ten yards away. The old bull stopped near him and sniffed the wind; then the animal moved on, toward the meadow. The hunter peered cautiously through the underbrush, and raised his bow as the last cow came into sight, busily cropping at every choice morsel of grass or leaf as she wandered after the others.

Ted held his bow steady and began to draw. The string strained and stretched as the arrow came back, and he could hear it squeak slightly under the tension. The feather touched his cheek and he held steady, aiming. There came the crack like a rifle shot and the cow leaped in fright. The elk all broke into a run, thundering away into denser trees; and Ted lowered his bow and gazed heartbrokenly at the broken string. The willow bark had dried too much, as he had known it would some time. But what a time! He had lost his chance to gain a good supply of meat, as well as the badly needed hide and sinew. Then he thought of the pistol. He had to get at least one animal, for it would provide sinew for a good bowstring. It was certainly worth one shot, anyway.

The pouch was filled with small game, but at the bottom lay the old pistol, and Ted dug it out as he ran. The elk would soon stop, and they were still headed for the meadow. Choosing a roundabout way, he tried to guess where he might come out, and leaping stumps and windfalls, he headed around the far side of the clearing.

Within fifteen minutes he was circling the little meadow from the opposite side to that where the elk would enter. His breath came in great gasps, but he tried to keep his panting from making too much noise as he looked through the screen of bushes into the meadow. The elk were not there! They must have moved on through, or past, the edge. He dropped to hands and knees and crept to the very edge of the meadow, still hidden by low bushes. His pistol was still gripped tightly in one hand, and as he knelt, he pointed it ahead, thumb ready to cock the weapon. A slight sound from across the clearing made him sink to his stomach, cocking the hammer at the same time. He was thankful for the impulse that made him do this, for even as the click of the cocking sounded faintly in the still air, the bull elk stepped into the clearing.

Ted lay silent and still on his stomach, and slowly he slid the pistol in front of him, gripping it with both hands as he lined up the sights. The bull advanced a step or two into the meadow, sensing danger yet not recognizing it. He turned toward the pile of roots Ted had laid out and took several steps toward it. The rest of the elk moved quietly out of the trees then, and the bull turned back toward the far side of the open space. He was about to disappear into the woods again, and Ted feared the whole band would get away, but one of the cows emerged from the bushes only a few yards away from the motionless boy. Quickly he lined up on her and squeezed the trigger.

For a long moment the sound of the explosion rolled through the trees, echoing from the rocks around. The grey smoke drifted across the clearing and gradually lifted. Ted lay where he was, ready to fire again if necessary; but there was no need. The heavy lead slug had caught the cow behind the shoulder, piercing her heart and dropping her in her tracks. There were no other elk to shoot at then. Ted rose and walked over to the fallen animal. He saw that she was dead, and lost no time in laying her out so that he could skin and cut up the carcass.

This job took him only a short while, compared to the first time he had tried it. He was bigger and stronger now, and well practised at the job. Long before dark he was finished and on his way back to the cave with all the meat he could carry. Using the skin as a packsack, he tied up nearly a hundred pounds of venison. At his cave he laid the meat inside and blocked up the door with stones to keep out passing scavengers while he went back for his pouch and bow and the roots.

With a pile of roots outside the cave and a good load of meat inside, he turned to some means of preserving the latter. Weaving a rough basket of evergreen branches, he climbed up the hill to the nearest snow patch and brought back all he could carry. After several such arduous trips he had a sufficient quantity of snow in one of the smaller caves, and there he stored the meat, except for the tongue and some other parts that he would eat immediately. The mouth of the storehouse was closed with slabs of stone.

On the following day he began treating the skin; and, with a good supply of tough sinews now on hand, he twisted and braided a fine new bowstring. The bow was strong and solid, and the string stretched like a steel rod across it. This one would not break.

His supper that night was cooked in a way he had learned from the Stony Indians—the way of cooking that had given the tribe its name. Near the fresh-water spring he dug a hole, which he lined with a piece of hide. Nearby he made a fire, and in it heated a number of stones; then he filled the hole with water, which he carried from the spring in his hunting pouch. Into the water went the elk tongue and a quantity of the edible roots. Using a couple of sticks, Ted now picked up some of the hot stones and dropped them into the water. Adding more stones from time to time, he was able to bring the water to the boil and cook his dinner.

Never had food tasted so good.

Chapter Fifteen

THE valley was noisy; Ted heard the sounds of life on all sides as he walked along. In the air birds of many kinds screamed, chirped, sang and whistled. Squirrels stuttered from treetop lookouts, and far up the scree slopes of the mountain echoed the long whistles of marmots. Ted turned toward the high rocks, looking up the steep slope to the white snowcap at the top. Almost before he realized it, he was walking toward the mountain.

He had always been fascinated by high peaks. He began to wonder what might be up there, high above the timber line, above his camp, above everything around him. How far could he see? What lay over the mountain, in the next valley? But at the first steep rise he stopped. How could he even think of spending the time so sorely needed for hunting? Wistfully he turned away from the magnificent sight.

A fresh trail drew his attention. Elk had passed this way

very recently. He followed, for surely the tracks would lead to a water hole, and such a spot was the best place to lie in wait for game. He had found that out long ago. He kept a careful watch on all sides as he stepped rapidly along. A dense patch of bush hid the trail from him at one point, but he ducked low and moved silently around it, and almost walked right over the elk which lay there.

Startled, he drew back and fumbled for bow and arrow. He could not realize for a moment what had happened. The animal lay still, legs sticking stiffly from the bloated carcass. Feeling a little foolish, Ted lowered his weapon and took stock of the scene. The elk had been killed only a few hours before, judging by the signs around. Ted inspected it carefully, interested to see what had made the kill. He thought first of bear, for he had seen much sign of them in other places and this looked like a bear kill. But then, why had it not been eaten? Usually the quarry would have been torn apart and most if not all eaten by the killer. And if the bear had not eaten it, the coyotes would have. He bent to look for tracks.

Almost immediately he found one good print in the dirt. But it was not that of a bear; at least, not a very large one. Another thing that puzzled the boy was the number of long, deep wounds in the back and sides of the elk, and shorter slashes at the shoulder. The throat of the slain animal had been ripped open, as though by a savage bite. Had the attacker been a bear, one blow from the heavy paw would serve to break the neck, and a bear would never rake the body that way. Ted thought over all his past experiences, but could find no answer to the problem. He walked on along the trail. The meat of the slain elk was rapidly spoiling in the sun, so he could not use any of it.

Other tracks caught his eye, and he continued on the same path as before, still hoping for water. He came upon the stream only a few hundred yards farther along. The water burbled and splashed over a rocky ledge, disappearing into the loose rockfall below, but at the top of the rock it formed a small pool. This was what Ted had been looking for, a water hole. Well-beaten trails led to it from several directions, but only one animal was in sight when the hunter reached it. That animal was a deer, and it was dead.

Blood still oozed from the torn throat and slashed loins, for it had been dead only a few minutes. It bore the same marks of butchery as the elk. What a pity, thought Ted. What kind of animal was in this valley, that would kill and leave good meat to rot? What savage beast would attack two animals the same day, and yet not eat? At least, Ted presumed it was the same killer. He searched the ground carefully for tracks. The edge of the stream was muddy, and there he found another clear print, the same shape and size as the one at the first kill. Then he found other tracks, all leading away from the carcass. But nowhere could he find tracks leading to it. How had the beast come upon the deer? Surely it did not come out of thin air.

Had Ted been superstitious, he might have turned and left the valley then, but something drew him on again, following the strange tracks. They led toward the rock of the mountain, upward to timberline. Often Ted lost the trail, to pick it up again after circling and searching with greatest care. It led him over logs and up rocks, where it seemed no animal could leap, save the mountain goat. And when he reached the bare rock at timberline, he lost the trail completely.

After an hour of search proved fruitless, he gave up, and raised his head to look at the mountains above him. It was then he realized that the day was gone. Night clouds were piling up overhead. Little light was left that day. Surprised at the lateness, Ted looked quickly around for a camp site, and chose a hollowed-out spot under the rock wall. He was just at the edge of timber, so that the wind-twisted and dead growth provided plenty of firewood. When he had his fire burning brightly, he ate some of the dried meat he had brought, wishing that he had not wasted the whole day in chasing something he had never seen and could not find. He lay thoughtfully under the cliff, well sheltered and warmed by the crackling fire. With his eyes closed, he still wondered about the beast he had trailed, and tried to imagine what it might be.

The scream that wakened him was ghastly in the still night air. He listened, and felt his neck shiver as it came again. It was like the scream of a horrified woman—or a man in great pain. Ted leaped to his feet, clutching for his bow. But when the sound rang out again and closer to him, he felt the thrill of real fright come over him. The fear of the unknown is terrible, and Ted stood where he was, not knowing what to do or where to go. He only knew that he wanted to run, but could not. For ten minutes he stayed almost still, close to his dying fire. Then when no further sounds came out of the darkness he found that he could move again, and hurriedly built up his fire. He did not know what was out there, but he knew that no animal on earth would brave the fire. Then he thought of his pistol, and dived for his pouch to get it.

For the rest of the night he sat with his back against the stone of the cliff, pistol in hand, feeding the fire to keep it hot and bright. When morning came he was tired, but the mystery kept him from being sleepy; and such a calm had descended over the whole mountain that he lost all his fear of the night. But his curiosity had doubled, and instead of starting back down the mountain, as he had sworn to do many times during the night, he knocked over a grouse that flew close to him, and his breakfast was soon made and eaten.

Almost before he had finished the last morsel of the bird, he was startled by another scream. This time it was so close that he leapt to his feet, eyes scanning the surrounding rocks, trying to catch sight of whatever had made the sound. Surely there could be no other human being so high on the mountain. But then, there was the possibility that a lone hunter, or even a small band, had followed goats up the rock. Had they met with trouble during the night? The screams were so human that Ted started searching for a way to get up the rocks to have a look.

A narrow crack in the rough face of the cliff allowed him room to clamber up the first part of the rock, until he came out onto a sloping ledge leading up and around the corner of the mountain. Slowly and carefully he stepped over the loose rock on the ledge, and by leaning against the cliff he found that he could walk fairly easily. The trail curved smoothly around a great bulge in the stone, and when he glanced down Ted saw that there was an almost vertical drop to the valley floor, a long way down. For a moment or two he stood against the cliff face, resting and searching for signs of life—or of death, for he was sure someone had been hurt or killed.

So suddenly did the trail end that Ted fell against the body that lay there. This time it was a goat, the kind Ted had watched so often in the evenings, as the animals wound their way in long lines up the steep slopes to high, safe hiding places. Here again the killer had struck. The goat's throat had been torn as had the others, and long slashes marked the back and sides. Ted felt a hot anger rising through him. This was senseless slaughter. Three fine game animals had died within a few hours, all for no purpose that the boy could understand. It seemed that whatever was doing the killing did so for pleasure, not for food as most beasts would. What kind of thing was on the mountain, then? What would kill and kill without eating more than a mouthful, and what would live this high up in the bare rocks?

The answer came almost as he was thinking. From a ledge a few feet above him came a scream that sent Ted leaping for cover. As he ducked, he felt rather than saw the huge shape flying through the air. The beast landed square upon the dead goat, gave a snarl of disappoinment, and disappeared in one bound over the edge of the rock.

For perhaps five minutes Ted crouched in the shelter of the cliff. He knew now what he was chasing—or rather, what had ended up chasing him. The tawny body, long snakelike tail and cat's face made him think of what he had heard from other hunters. This was a panther, also known as a mountain lion or cougar. It was called a dozen names by the Indians, who feared the big cat even more than they did the grizzly bear.

The panther was the only animal save the wolf that killed for the joy of killing; and like the wolf, it was despised by Indian and white man alike. Ted remembered tales of how one would wait on a limb or ledge until his prey walked underneath. Then would come the leap, the clutching talons on the shoulders, the kicking hind feet that tore great gashes in the back, and finally the snap of fangs at the throat. One bite, one mouthful, that was all the killer wanted. Such an animal could not be left to roam this valley. Ted needed the game himself, if he was to get through the winter. He would have to kill the panther.

He waited until he heard the terrifying scream, and followed the direction of the sound. All that day he followed, without getting close. The cat was playing with him, he decided. So he selected a sheltered ledge and sat down, ears and eyes alert and pistol ready, to wait until the cougar should come to him.

He did not have long to wait. The killer was curious, and angry at the intruder. The light wind had dropped away almost altogether, and in the silence Ted caught the faint scraping of claws on rock, and the soft pad-pad of cushioned paws. From the sound he could estimate just about where the beast would come into sight, and he raised the pistol at arm's length, holding it cocked and ready to line up instantly.

The green eyes and snarling mouth seemed to cover the whole face of the mountain lion; and at the same time that the head appeared, the full blast of its scream made Ted stumble backward, fumbling to bring his gun in line. Without another sound the cat leaped. As it lifted from its place and floated upward, Ted threw himself against the cliff, aimed and fired. He shrank against the wall as the roar blasted out, filling the day with thunder and covering the whole scene with a pall of smoke. The cat landed beside the lad, scrambling to regain its balance and turn to face its attacker. Before it could spring again, Ted fired another shot directly into the hate-filled face. The second shot was enough. With a little whimper, the killer sank back on its haunches, settled softly on the rock and died.

Ted felt a stinging in one arm, and was surprised to find that several long scratches were bleeding. The claws of the cat must have touched him as it fell past, but the marks were not serious. The claws, though, would make another fine necklace some day.

While the pounding of his heart gradually slowed, Ted rested and examined his kill; then he skinned it and rolled the carcass over the edge of the cliff. The meat was no good to eat, and he would have enough to carry with the thick pelt and tail. He rolled it and tied it to his back. The day was passing and it was time to get down while there was still light. On the way, Ted passed one of the slaughtered animals, thrilling to the thought that this monster, at least, would kill no more.

Close to his camp he came upon another water hole, and surprised a small deer. It took three arrows and a little trailing to finally bring it down, after which he took the hide and sinews and some choice parts. With such a load he made slow time back up the hill to his cave, but somehow he got there.

That meat lasted him for a few days, until he could get out in the valley and shoot two more elk for his larder. Loaded down with venison, he made trip after trip until his snow cave was filled. Another day he took to dress the hides and make up his tanning mash. The sinews were soaked and hung in the cave for future use. A pile of dead wood grew on one side of the cave as he dragged in every dead tree he could find close by.

And then one night, while Ted slept, winter came to the mountains.

Chapter Sixteen

THE snow piled high around Ted's cave, and he was glad that he was ready for it. His storage cave was well stocked with meat, and firewood was abundant. He ran out of roots very quickly, but managed to dig a few more close to the hot spring; and these he rationed to himself sparingly.

Most of the time there was not much to do, and he was restless. He waited impatiently for the time when he could leave the fortress of the mountains and make his way back to Fort Edmonton, to let his mother and father know that he was safe. There was the farm to build, and so much to do. He counted the days as they slowly passed, hoping for an early thaw, a long chinook—any lessening of the winter that would allow him to travel without too much trouble.

Finally the snow fell for the last time, and gentle rain took its place. Little by little the brown hills emerged from the high white tepees of snow. As soon as he could see the grass, Ted went down into the valley and searched until he found more of the bulbous roots. He longed for the flour and tea and salt that he had been forced to do without for so long.

Now that the long winter was at an end, he sat on the bare hillside and watched spring come to the mountains. In the deep valleys the snow was still ten or fifteen feet deep, and too soft to walk over. He could only wait. And while he waited, his twentieth birthday came and went, and Ted did not even know it. He forgot everything but his eagerness to be up and travelling.

The wind that swept out of the north grew weak, and soon stopped. It gave way to a warm wind from the west, and Ted could stay no longer. He packed what dried meat he had left, slung his pouch, and took his bow and arrow. The hot spring still bubbled and fumed as he passed it for the last time and headed directly south into the midday sun, into the wilderness of peaks and hills that lay before him.

He followed the stream through the valley and through gaps in the hills, until he came to a place where it joined another creek, and together the two made a small river that ran swiftly southward.

Passing along a high bank above the river, Ted happened to look down into a pool, and deep in the icy water he caught the silver gleam of a fish. Fish! It was so long since he had eaten one that he had almost forgotten what it was like.

The fish he had seen was a large one; and as he watched he saw several others darting about. Occasionally one would make a lunge upwards, breaking the surface of the water. They were jumping at small bits of floating grass and wood; and Ted formed a plan. He cut a tiny bit of meat from a strip of dried venison, and with his bow ready, tossed it in. As soon as the meat struck the water there came an explosion, and the bait was gone. Ted stared foolishly at the widening rings.

He would have to do it differently. He notched another arrow, and laid the bow down while he cut another piece of bait. Then he picked up the bow and arrow, holding the meat in the hand that grasped the bow. With a quick movement he flipped the bow upwards, making the bait fly out and into the water, at the same time drawing the arrow sharply with his other hand. By the time the meat fell into the water, he was standing ready, arrow drawn, waiting for the strike. When it came he released his arrow instantly, but it struck the water far from the fish. He had to get closer, straight above if possible.

He walked along the shore a few yards, to where a fallen tree jutted out above the water. Here the water was smooth and clear, and he could see the stones in the bottom. The run-off snow had not yet begun to bring down its load of silt, and every pebble shone in the sunlight. There were no fish below him, but he knew how to fix that. A piece of meat tossed upstream brought another splash. Another bit tossed a little closer, a short wait, and then the splash. By throwing the bait shorter and shorter each time, Ted gradually drew the fish downstream until he could again see them, and finally they were directly below him.

He chopped a piece of meat into tiny bits and threw them into the water. They struck the surface, and the water churned as the trout went after them. Ted noticed that they struck at every piece he dropped, and that they went after everything else too. But when they came after a piece of wood or grass, they would merely nose it and swim away, often close to the surface. He dropped a few more pieces of bait, and readied his bow again. Then into the water he dropped a twig. His arrow was pointed straight down now, and when a trout dashed up after the twig, turned and started to swim away, Ted shot.

The water frothed white, then red, and Ted let out a yell as he saw his arrow borne away. It was lost, and so was the fish. Determined to beat this problem, he took from his pouch the roll of sinews he carried at all times. They were dry and hard, but he laid them in the water for a few minutes. That water was like ice, and he did not hold his hands in for long, but soon the fibres were soft and pliable, and he stuck them in his mouth to keep them so while he began tying them together into a long line.

When the string was about ten feet long, he tied one end to an arrow, near the feathers, and the other end he tied around his wrist. With the coil hanging loosely from his hand, he baited the water again; and this time when he shot, the fish swam only to the end of the line and Ted pulled it back and onto shore in a matter of seconds. Three more of the larger trout he secured in this way: then he built a fire, cooked two of the fish, and had a delicious meal. The other two he cleaned and packed in dry grass, for they would make a good supper.

Without wasting any more time Ted started downstream, and with every stop now he felt more and more certain that this country was familiar. When he rounded a hill and saw the bend in the river, he was sure. The stream had turned into a good-sized river, and now it changed direction and headed straight east, toward the prairies. There, only a few miles farther on, was the sharp

vee of the gateway, the opening in the mountains where it
flowed through to the plains, right down to Spitzee Anota.
This was the Spitzee River, and Ted had travelled it many
times. From where he stood he could now recognize all the
hills. And right over there, not two miles away, was the
hill where he had built his snug home and lived for three
years. He had been within twenty miles of it all the time.

Ted felt the urge to see his old dugout again. The old
trail was still there, though partly covered with snow. No
hunters had been along it so early in the year, and Ted
was careful not to walk close to it, for he did not want his
footprints to be spotted by the keen-eyed Indians. He
skirted the trail and climbed upward until he was near the
top of the hill. Then he started walking around it, and
when he had come almost to the west side, he reached his
camp.

The place was as though he had just come in from the
day's hunt, as though he had never left it. Nothing had
been touched in the year since he had last seen it. No man
or animal had tried the stone-and-log barricade of the
door, and only a few tracks showed in the dirt around the
site. Ted did not stop to enter. He felt that he must hurry
along, out onto the plains to find a horse and make his way
back to Edmonton. He turned away and headed east, down
the hill, along the river bottom, out through the tall vee of
the pass, out into the plains.

Spring was everywhere. In the mountains the snow still
lay deep in valleys and forests, but out in the open there
was little to show that the ground had been covered only a
few days before. Peace seemed to settle over the whole
world again. Ted's feeling of restless urgency fell away,
and he rested often and long as he made his way down-

stream along the river. He recognized the trail and the landmarks that still showed him his way. On the fifth day since leaving his winter camp he came to the region of the Spitzee crossing.

His first sight of the district was from the high bank overlooking the island. There, proudly alone in their clearing, stood the Medicine Trees, the great bough that joined them forming a stately arch. In front of them and to one side, the yellow-brown logs of the fort rose ugly and dark against the light-brown grass. There was no sound save the dashing of water in the river. There was no movement but the ripple of the long grass. He watched from a hiding-place, but no human came, no danger showed.

Ted crossed the river and approached the fort; and it was not until he was close to the wall that he saw the reason the place was silent. The roofs of the buildings were gone, the logs stuck up from the corners, blackened and bare. The fort had been burned again. He went into the compound to look for any sign or trace to show what tribe had done it. He was not sorry; it had been a bad place, where evil men had fought and killed, and traded poisonous whiskey to the natives. He hoped that it would not be rebuilt.

Discovering nothing from the ruin, Ted turned to the crossing; and once on the south side, he soon picked up the trail that led back to the clearing where they had built their cabin. When he came in sight of the place his heart gave a leap, for here they had built more than a house. Here they had built their dreams for the future.

The remains of the trading post were black against the grass, and almost overgrown. It was over four years since it had been burned, and nearly a year since the last time

Ted had seen it. He stood looking at it for a long time. He gazed around the clearing, and began to make plans. Here, he thought, would be the best place for the house. Not a one-roomed cabin this time, but a real house, of squared logs, with two rooms downstairs and two upstairs, and a big kitchen with a great stone fireplace where his mother might do her work in warmth and cheerful brightness. And real glass in the windows; and sturdy homemade chairs and bedsteads and table.

And over there by the creek would be the barn, where their horses would be safe from attack by wolves or Indians, and if they were able to buy a yoke of oxen and some cows, they would have plenty of room for them. Later on, with pigs, chickens and geese, they would have the grandest farm in all of Assiniboia, in all of Canada.

But they could not settle for a while yet. He and his father and René Corteau would have to come here, and clear more land for the fields, and raise the buildings. There was a great deal to do, and he knew there was no time to lose in dreaming. He had to get a horse somewhere and ride to Edmonton to bring out the others.

The best thing to do, he decided, was to go to the crossing and travel along close to the trail. Even if he walked all the way, it would not take more than a couple of weeks at the most. He had no fear of the Indians now, for they would be too busy finding food after the winter. If he kept close to the trail to Edmonton, there was a good chance he would meet a party of hunters or traders going north, and be able to get a mount, or at least a ride.

So he crossed the river again and moved north, sometimes walking, sometimes running a little way. That night he camped within sight of the Okotoks, the big rock where

he had been captured the year before. There was no sign
of the Blackfeet now; they had been driven away and their
camp destroyed. He wasted no time grieving for them, but
continued on across the low hill country until the next
night brought him to a large river. Here he camped for the
night; and next morning he saw the riders.

He watched from cover as they approached. There were
about twenty in the band, and some were Indians. But most
of them wore white men's clothing, and rode in saddles.
They did not look like white men, though; and it was only
at the last minute, when they were almost past him, that
he recognized their leader. It was La Nouse, the half-breed
hunter and trapper, who made this trip many times each
year. Ted had met him at Edmonton, had hunted with
him, and knew him for one of the finest people of the
plains.

He hopped from his cover and gave a loud yell. The party
stopped and Ted ran forward, shouting in English, Stony
and Blackfoot, forgetting for the moment just what language La Nouse spoke. Weapons were raised, and Ted
halted and gave the sign of peace. The rifles fell away, and
he approached. When La Nouse saw who it was he was
overjoyed, for he and Ted were good friends.

So Ted joined the half-breed's band, borrowed the use
of a pony, and in four days more was in Fort Edmonton.
The first thing he did when they entered the big gate was
to ride directly to the cabin where his mother lived. After
he had rushed in to surprise her, he gave the horse back to
its owner and walked across the compound to greet his
father. Corteau saw him first and rushed upon him like a
small bear. His father did the same; and then they trouped
to the cabin, where Ted told his story. That night there was

a great celebration supper. The family was all together again.

"Father, we must go to Spitzee right away," Ted said, as they sat around the fire. "We have so much to do before we can start farming. We have to clear more of the fields so that we can plant grain, and there is a barn to build, and fences——"

"Hold on, Son." James put up a hand, smiling at the eagerness in the boy's voice and eyes. "We have a lot to do, all right, and we will have to get started, as you say. The only thing is, will your mother agree to stay here in Edmonton while we work at Spitzee?" The trio of men looked silently at the woman, and in a moment she nodded.

"Aye, James, I'll stay and wait. I know I'll only be in the way while you're cleaning up, but just as soon as you've got the cabin built, come for me."

"We'll come, Mother," vowed Ted.

"Ah, oui, we weel come for you, I'm t'eenk," René put in. "Ain't no man w'at don' like for have woman to cook good meal for heem. We come to gat you, dat's plenty certain, eh Ted?"

They laughed with him, and the plans took shape that night. The next few days saw them gather tools and materials for the trip, and within two weeks they were rolling out of Edmonton once again, along the now familiar trail to Spitzee.

Chapter Seventeen

THE site of the old trading post was almost hidden in
the long, dry grass. Ted could hardly see where the
walls had been. Corteau stepped down from his pony to
kick at the burned logs that remained.

"I'm t'ink she's got leetle hole in de roof," he said with
a wide smile. "Ol' Corteau, he's get plenty wet in dis
cabin." James and the boy chuckled as they dismounted.

"Yes, René, I guess we'll have to rebuild it. There's
surely not much left." He picked up a piece of rusted
metal. "It's a wonder they didn't cover the whole place.
They usually do when they want to destroy a campsite.
They must be getting lazy."

Ted had been poking about among the ruins of the
corral, and in one corner he came upon several empty
powder kegs that they had once used as water buckets.

"Look here, Father!" he cried. "All the bands have

rusted off these kegs." He kicked at the kegs and they fell to pieces.

"No, no, Ted, my fren'," corrected Corteau. "Dey are not rust off. De Injun, he's take all de metal he fin'. Make heem better arrow point an' spear point dan de bone and stone, eh Jeem?"

"Right, René," agreed James. "The natives pick up every bit of iron and steel, and they file it or work it into knives and points and all kinds of tools that they used to make from stone and bone. It's a wonder they didn't take this too." He held out the object he had picked up. It was a large buckle, probably from a belt.

"Dat's de one t'ing Injun got no use for." Corteau took the buckle from MacDonnell, turning it over and looking closely at it. "Dis buckle, hees not beeg enough for make not'eeng wit', an' w'en de Injun want to fasten belt, he's jus' tie heem up. She's not good for not'eeng, dees wan." He flipped the piece into the grass behind him.

"Well, come on, lads. Let's be at it!" James tied his pony to a willow clump and began to unpack the tools. The others followed his lead and in a few minutes the grassy clearing once again echoed to the ring of axes as they began clearing the bushes and saplings which had grown up around the cabin site.

Suddenly James stopped his work. A look of deep thought creased his forehead.

"W'at's de matter, Jeem?" called Corteau from across the clearing.

"I just thought of something," James answered. "Ted, René, stop work and come over here for a minute."

"What's wrong, Father?" asked Ted, growing a little

worried at the expression on his father's face. "What are we stopping for? Is something the matter?"

"I just thought of something important. We can't build the cabin and barns here." Both his son and his friend stared at him in astonishment.

"Why not, Father?"

"Because I remember three wet and miserable men who had to perch all night in these trees," he answered, grinning impishly at Corteau. The Frenchman gasped at the memory.

"Sacré nom de nom!" he cried. "For certain we can't build heem here. Mebbe again she's come de flood. Ol' Corteau, he's get drown for sure nex' time. Jeem, we got to move her to higher lan', de cabin, eh?"

"Yes, René, that's what I mean." Ted was laughing as his father spoke, and both MacDonnells could not help making fun of the small man's great dislike for water. If there was any water around, he was sure to fall into it.

"That's what I mean," James repeated. "We'll have to build up on the bench somewhere, but we can clear this land and use it for pasture or plough it up for crops. It's good land and should grow wheat well."

"Father!" Ted gave a sudden cry. "I know just the place to build the house and barns. Up on the bank a little ways. There's a sort of shelf just above the trees, and it's plenty big enough for the cabins. It's below the edge of the bank too, and ought to be protected from the wind. I saw it when I was hunting there when we built the first cabin."

"Where is it, Son?" James took the boy's word, for he knew that Ted had explored every part of this valley when they had first camped there. If there was any place suitable for building, the lad would know where to find it. "Can you take us there now?" he asked.

"Oh yes, Father. It's only a little way."

They went toward the hill, through the thick brush, and approached the little creek that separated them from the south bank of the old river bed, rising thirty feet above the bottom lands. The whole area was covered with tall poplar trees, and the spaces were crowded with clumps of willow and service-berry bushes.

"Sure lots of beaver around here now," commented James, pointing to the white-topped stumps of trees. Piles of yellow chips lay scattered like leaves all around them.

"Look at the channels they've dug to float their cuttings to the creek," said Ted.

They had to step over several of the long trenches before they came to the edge of the tiny stream, which was perhaps ten or twelve feet wide at this point. Ted walked to a place where several large stones rose above the water and stepped lightly out on them, jumping from one to another. As he neared the other side, his foot struck a loose stone and he went in the water up to his ankle.

"Come on!" he called, seeing the others hesitate.

James followed his son, and in a moment was beside him. Then both looked at the French-Canadian, who still stood on the far side of the creek.

"Oh, come on, René!" urged James. "Take a chance. There's only the one loose stone in the lot. You can't get very wet, anyway—the water's only a foot deep here."

"No, no," cried René. "Ol' Corteau, he's try dat, he's get plenty wet, for certain. Dis French fellow he's gone to find better way, I'm bet yo'."

So saying, he began to search up and down the creek

bank, until he caught sight of just the tree he was looking for. It was a willow, nearly twenty feet high, he guessed, which when bent down would reach across the water nicely. He started to climb it, his back to the stream; and as he went higher the tree began to bend, until it bowed far out across the water. Now Corteau swung himself around to face the opposite bank and swung himself hand over hand along his impromptu bridge, holding his feet high above the water.

The leafy top of the willow touched the far bank, and Corteau pulled himself up among its branches and held on to them to steady himself as he walked the rest of the way.

Corteau was not one to let this moment of triumph pass unnoticed. With a shout he stood up on the branch and raised both arms.

"Look, my fren's!" he called to Ted and James. "W'en yo' are in de beeg wood, yo' got to be plenty smart, like me. I'm cross de creek an' I'm not get wet, I'm bet yo', eh?" And he bent his knees to jump to dry land.

"No, René, don't jump!" yelled Ted.

"René—you'd better not——" But James could not finish for laughing.

Corteau ignored both pleas, as though he had not heard. He leaped from his swaying perch onto the grassy bank below. The tree swooshed upward, and Corteau swooshed downward. Before he could utter a word, he sank to his waist in the soft earth of the bank. He had jumped right on top of a beaver tunnel, and had broken through. Both Ted and James doubled up with mirth as they watched, waiting for the explosion they knew would follow.

The suddenness of his plunge, the feel of soft mud around his thighs, the bite of cold water as it soaked through his moccasins and leggings and rose around him, made him draw in a deep breath of shock. But once he had realized what had happened, he let go.

"Sacré nom de petit cochon bleu!" he screamed, and beat the grass with both fists. "Nom de nom de nom! Eef dees fellow, hees got to be half de fish, den he be *all* de fish." And he dragged himself from the muddy hole and leaped, arms and legs flailing, into the middle of the creek.

Ted could hardly stand, he laughed so hard. James felt the tears rolling down his cheeks, and the howls of glee must surely have frightened away all the game in the valley. But finally they were able to hold back their sobs of laughter long enough to help René climb from the water. Wet and dripping and completely dejected, he watched his friends with utter disgust.

He was a very unhappy man for a while, but James took his arm and the two old friends followed Ted, who had started out ahead. The three made their way through the wood, silent now save for the sloppy squishing of Corteau's moccasins.

Presently they reached the place that Ted remembered. The bank formed a sort of shelf here, jutting out from the high river wall, and the flat area was quite large enough for all the buildings they would ever need. The only trouble was that there were not many trees around for building material. They inspected every inch of the field, laying out the boundaries where their fences would run; and when they had the yard planned, they marked off the corners of the house.

This was not to be any rough cabin, but a regular house of logs, fit for the woman who would rule it in a little while. It was to be the headquarters of the MacDonnell farm, the first of many such buildings that in time would arise across this wild land.

During the building of their old post Ted had been too small to do any heavy work, but now he found that most of the toughest chores became rather enjoyable as he worked the rough-barked trunks. Before they cut even the first log, the three men had decided that none of the trees around the cabin site would be touched for building purposes. So they cleared trails through the underbrush along the stream, and used the horses to drag the logs from the lower part of the valley, where they would have to cut trees to clear their fields anyway. It took them a week of steady work to cut and drag up enough logs to make a start on the cabin.

The first logs—twenty feet long for the front and back, twelve for the sides—were laid on a foundation of stones. Each log was rolled close to the position it would occupy, and rough preliminary notches were cut at each end. Then it was lifted into place, and the curves of the logs below it were marked above the notches. After this it was taken down again and the notches rounded out to the indicated curves. Two or three fittings were necessary before the correct depth and shape were reached; then the log was put into place for the last time. As a result of this careful work, the logs fitted at the corners without so much as a crack between them.

After each one was in place, the third man took a big auger and drilled three or four holes down through it at the joint, right into the log below it. Into these holes he drove long wooden pegs, to hold the walls solid and square. Two by two the logs were laid, across the sides, then the ends, then the sides again, until the walls had reached the

desired height. After the last pair of side logs was in position, the end walls were brought up level by means of half
logs, cut flat top and bottom and pegged in several places
to the logs below, which had also been cut flat to receive
them.

During this construction the horses came into use again.
As the walls rose higher, getting the heavy side logs into
position became increasingly difficult. They solved the
problem by placing several sturdy poles against the wall
to serve as skids, then putting rope slings around the logs
and running the ropes right across the cabin to the other
side, where they were hitched to the horses. It then became
a simple matter to haul the timbers into place.

Before the roof could be put on, the doors and windows
had to be cut. Their keen axes made short work of cutting
out the top log of each opening, and then their long saw
came into play. One by one the sections of logs dropped to
the ground as the sharp blade whined back and forth,
spewing yellow sawdust in little heaps at their feet. Slabs
were split off short logs and fastened along the inside of
the openings to hold the log ends secure until proper frames
could be installed.

Then they started on the roof. First a series of poles was
nailed to the top logs across the width of the house, to
serve as joists for the ceiling they would build later. Next
they chose a sturdy timber to serve as the ridgepole, and
cut it square—no mean job in itself. Several logs of the
approximate lengths required were cut flat on top and
bottom, placed together, and marked in a triangle to form
one of the gable ends; then they were cut to size, and the
smallest one was notched to receive the ridgepole. They
were then hoisted into position in turn, and each one

firmly pegged to the one below it. The other gable end was cut and installed in the same way.

Now came the engineering feat of getting the ridgepole into place. Ropes were run across the tops of the gable ends, from one side of the building to the other. Heavy spikes guided them, and the wood over which they ran was liberally greased to cut down friction. The skid poles were leant against the side of the house again, and once more the horses provided the hauling power. At one gable end, mounted on a strong though crudely made ladder, was Ted, while his father perched at the other gable. Together they guided the ridgepole into place.

A supply of rafters had already been prepared, using one as a pattern for all the others to insure uniformity. The upper ends of these logs were bevelled to fit against the ridgepole, and rough semicircles were cut near the other ends to fit over the top logs of the side walls. They were placed close together, to support the sod roof, fireproof and weatherproof, that would finish off the structure.

"I don't suppose your mother will mind a sod roof, just for a few years until we get time to make a supply of shakes," said James. "After all, she's gone through much worse before this."

For three weeks more they laboured from dawn to dusk, daubing and chinking the logs, hanging the doors, framing windows, even though there was no glass for them as yet. Perhaps they would be able to bring out some sheets the next year. But until then, skin would have to do.

Inside the cabin the great fireplace dominated one end, and the other end was partitioned off into two tiny cubicles, one for James and his wife, the other for Ted and René. The furnishings would come later, but first there were other things to attend to. So long as the men had food and shelter they cared little for other comforts. The land called, and they began to spend long hours each day in cutting and hauling away brush from around the cabin. Trees that might make good building logs were stacked to one side, while stumps and trash were burned. When the oxen arrived from Edmonton they could begin ploughing the flat prairie land on the bench, but first this farmyard had to be cleaned up and put in shape.

Often, as they laboured, they could see the silent forms of Indians moving through the trees. They would come to the edge of the clearing and stand watching for hours, silent and disapproving, knowing that where one man settled others would soon follow. These natives were Stonies, friends to Ted and his family, and sometimes they offered skins and clothing in trade for powder and shot. In this way the whites gathered a pile of furs with which to buy the supplies they would need soon. Often Ted asked about his friend, White Calf, but learned only that the band of Broken Shield was far west in the big shining hills.

Working steadily, the men piled up a good supply of building material, and yard by yard they pushed back the edge of the clearing, cutting deep into the dense brush and undergrowth that formed the heart of the old forest. This land was level and rich, for it was ancient river bed and covered with a deep layer of good black soil. The years of growth above it had left a layer of natural fertilizer which, when turned under, would grow practically anything.

Finally they grew tired of clearing, and moved back to the upper part of the farm, using some of their logs to build a fence and erect a long, low shelter that would form part of the stable. On the field below they left heaps of brush smouldering around the few stumps that had to be left in the ground. Some of the great trees could not be uprooted and must either be burned out or wait until oxen could be hitched to them.

Finally they reached the end of their labours for that season. While there was plenty they could have done, they felt satisfied that it could wait another year, for with work animals it would take only half the time and effort. No Indians came near now, and Ted thought how strange it was that this valley, which once echoed to the sounds from a thousand tents, now was empty. He remembered the white men's trading post up the river, and the hundreds of innocent Indians who had died from the traders' evil practices. Also, he knew that the buffalo were nearly gone from the plains, and what natives were left were no doubt out chasing them, or far to the west, in the mountains, hunting elk and deer.

There was not much game left in this valley now, but there would be enough to keep their little family going for a long time. In a few years they would raise cattle, pigs and chickens and would be almost self-sufficient. It seemed a pity that the day of the Indians was past, but that was progress and this country was growing up. It could no longer hold back the outside world.

When the last brush pile had burned and the men were ready to start back to Edmonton, Ted felt the old yearning run through him. He wanted to explore more country while the weather was good.

"Father," he said that day, "you and René go on to the fort, and I'll catch up with you along the way. I want to go south a little way to see if I can find any trace of White Calf."

"I'm glad you still think of your friend, Son," James told him. "But if you want to go south, then René and I will wait here for you. We can do with a bit of a rest, eh René?"

"But yes, my fren'. Ol' Corteau, he ees like dat idea. Eat and sleep all day. Mebbe catch some feesh too, eh? My, dat be fine t'ing, I'm t'eenk."

"Good!" laughed Ted. "You wait here, then, until I get back. I'll only be gone for two or three days, I should think. I just want to look over the land and try to get on White Calf's trail if I can. Well, I've got about all I need right here, I guess. Sure wish I had my old rifle, though, but I guess this one will do."

He hefted the shiny new breech-loader and slung it across his pony. Then he turned the horse's head up the hill and, with a wave of his arm, rode away.

Chapter Eighteen

Ted walked his pony to the top of a rise and looked southward. Nothing moved except the long prairie grass. Nothing made sound but the wind. Then to the southward a black speck slanted to the ground. Another followed, and in moments more specks wheeled and dropped behind the hills. Ted could not see what kind of birds they were, but he could see that they were large, and very dark. He reined the pony toward the spot and trotted off in that direction.

Long before he reached the place he knew what the birds were. In increasing numbers they flapped and soared from all directions, heading directly for the gathering. In dozens and scores they came, and from the ones that flew directly overhead, Ted could recognize the great black shapes of ravens and crows, and spotted here and there across the sky were the purple and white flashes of magpies. All were scavengers, eaters of the dead, and all were headed toward the same place on the prairie. Ted dug his heels into the pony's ribs and they sped across the grass at a steady run.

Almost before he knew it, they were upon the rim of a wide coulée, and Ted came near to losing his seat as the horse scrambled down the bank. Across the coulée the walls rose steeply at several points, topped by high ridges of grey stone. It was under one of these ridges that the birds were feasting. From the smell that rose Ted figured that the carcasses had been there for some time, perhaps several weeks.

This was a buffalo pound, and must have been run simply for hides, for whole animals still lay at the bottom of the cliff, and many more were being stripped of flesh by bird and beast alike. At Ted's approach the ravens and other birds rose like a great black cloud, filling the air with their raucous cries, while from the centre of the pile of bodies several yellow prairie wolves streaked for the cover of the rocks.

At the bottom of the coulée Ted's pony suddenly sank deep in black gumbo. The floor of the valley, knee-deep in grass, was quite marshy, and Ted saw open water a little farther on. He turned his horse and went around it. "Hah," he thought to himself, "René missed this one."

Once across the boggy valley, Ted halted to look for some way to get to the top. He knew that this run must be close to the buffalo migration route, and if so, then there was certainly some natural draw leading down and across the deep coulée. A hundred yards to the west of the heap of dead animals, he spotted it.

Another dried stream ran down to the valley floor, and the bottom of this draw was trampled and beaten down to a depth of three feet in some places, showing that this had been a regular route for the buffalo in their never-ending march up and down the country. Ted turned up this trail and in a little while it led him up the bank and out onto the prairie.

He looked back to the top of the rocks, where the buffalo had run over. Away from the smooth slab of stone that marked the drop, twin lines of cairns led outward onto the plains, making the familiar huge vee that ended with the small end at the cliff. There could be no doubt that this was a popular route for small bands of buffalo, and some tribe had camped close by, waiting until the beasts had come in sight. They had built up these long lines of heaps of stone, and probably had used them for many years. When a herd was sighted, it was driven into the trap and slaughtered.

Ted rode to the slab of rock and eased his pony to the edge. From the top he counted up to a hundred bodies, and knew that many others lay underneath these, and scores of already stripped skeletons showed that the mass killing had been a very successful bit of work. Holding his breath against the awful stench, he drew back away from the place, and once again turned toward the south.

The prairie was brown and very dry. Everywhere he looked there was grass, in many places touching the belly of his horse. The freshening wind rippled the whole countryside and Ted pushed his mount forward through the tangled growth. Far ahead he noticed clouds beginning to build up along the horizon, and the mountains began to disappear in haze. At a tiny stream he paused to chew on a strip of jerked meat, drinking from the warm, nearly stagnant water. His pony stood rigid, head up, as though alert for some danger, Ted noticed, and searched the flat lands all around, but could see nothing to alarm him. He pushed on a few miles farther before nightfall.

That night he slept on a low hilltop, under the stars. His pony grazed, hobbled in the Indian fashion. There was not so much long grass on the top of the hill, and it provided him with a good lookout position to all directions. He had picked this point because, heeding the actions of his horse, he feared some kind of trouble threatening. He slept with one hand on his rifle, and his ears tuned for any hint of attack.

Ted was awakened in the darkness some time before morning by the snorting and kicking of his horse. The pony had wandered, hopping in his hobbles, a short way down the hill, and Ted ran after him to lead him back.

When he saw the animal's frenzied struggles as it tried to run, the boy realized that something was wrong; and a deep breath told him what it was. Even before he ran back to the top of the hill and saw the glow, he knew the answer —the grass was on fire. Far away to the south the whole prairie was burning, or so it looked to the frightened lad. The horizon was a long line of fire, and the wind was rising out of the south. It would sweep the flames for miles before it died; and Ted was right in their path.

He threw his gear across the horse and leaped upon the beast's back, holding him in a little as they jumped down the slope and headed north, away from the fire. He let the pony have its head as much as he dared, hoping that it would be sure-footed enough not to fall in the darkness, and hoping also that dawn was not far off.

As the wind rose the smoke increased, until they seemed to be riding in a fog, and the pony could hardly tell hole from rock as it stumbled through the night. Each time Ted looked backward the glow of the oncoming fire seemed brighter. It was moving much faster than horse and rider. When the wind died a little, the roar of the flames came to him. He bent low over the pony's neck, coughing a little as he breathed.

A few minutes more brought a brightening to the sky, and Ted rejoiced to see that daylight was coming. And day did come at last, although there was not much sunlight. "This is as bad as a blizzard," thought Ted, for the sun burned a deep, bloody red in the east, and the countryside was blotted out by swirling smoke.

They passed the tiny creek where Ted had stopped to eat the day before, and it was there that he gained some hope. Only a few miles to the buffalo run, to the marshes. With the coming of light he had kicked his horse into a dead run and they ploughed through the thickening air, stumbling and plunging over banks and up rises, choking with every breath. The wind shrieked in harmony with the roar of the fire, throwing pieces of burning grass far ahead, so that even the air was filled with flame, and small, raging fires sprang up far in advance of the main conflagration, racing ahead of the refugees.

Now they began to catch up with other victims. Coyotes and rabbits in uncounted numbers dashed headlong before the terror. Birds flew up from their cover in the grass, some to stagger ahead through the smoke and to safety in the air above. Others flew blindly back into the searing furnace, and were dead before they fell. Most of the ground dwellers were caught up in the inferno, for they knew no place of safety but their own dens, and they were loath to leave, seeking refuge in the depths of nests and holes. Wolves darted past from all sides, and gophers scuttled to their deepest burrows, many to die of suffocation as the dead air rolled into their dens.

Even the burning of the trading post had not stirred Ted or frightened him as did the prairie fire. This fire spread across a whole country, many miles wide, and consumed everything in its path. Only when it was quenched by rain or turned back upon itself by a change of wind would it stop. Only those who were fortunate enough to gain shelter in bodies of water would survive. All creatures of the prairie were fleeing to refuge before the fiery storm, and Ted soon lost track of all else save the burning of his lungs and the hoarse, sobbing breaths of his pony as it laboured onward through the red cloud. Sparks landed on all sides, and the boy's shirt became spotted with brown, while the smell of burned hair reached his nostrils as the embers landed on the horse.

Suddenly, through all the misery of his flight, another thought struck Ted. The cliff! Plunging recklessly forward like this, unable to see more than a few feet ahead, suppose they ran over the edge? The thought made Ted sit up a little higher and look a little harder for any landmarks that might show him how close they were to the drop. A lean grey wolf, pelt smoking, half mad with pain and fear, raced past. It was almost out of sight in the smoke, perhaps thirty feet ahead, when it disappeared with a howl of fright. With a wild cry, Ted reined the pony sharply to the left; and even as the horse responded, he caught sight of the flat shelf of rock at the top of the drop.

The horse's hooves skidded on stone as it wheeled; it made a desperate leap to the side, and Ted came loose from his seat. He fell on the lip of the cliff, and the horse jumped down the face of the hill and was lost in the smoke.

Ted's breath was knocked out of him, and for a few moments he lay there half conscious. Then he opened his eyes, and saw the flames reaching out for him.

With all the strength he had left, he pushed himself away from the fire; and even though his body seemed broken in half, he rolled over the edge. He dropped about eight feet onto a grassy slope, and rolled the rest of the way to the bottom of the bank.

As the first flames licked the rim of the cliff, they seemed to hesitate. Then they leaped downward, following wherever there was enough grass to burn on either side of the pile of dead buffalo. By this time, however, Ted had managed to crawl to the water, and he pulled himself forward until it was deep enough to cover him, then rolled over and lay on his back, only his nostrils above the surface. All around him animals rolled or leaped into the pond, hunters and hunted huddling together from the common danger.

The flames reached the edge of the marsh, and even the wet grass began to steam and shrivel, while clouds of steam billowed up. Briefly the advance of the fire was checked; then the wind carried sparks to the dry grass on the other side, and the fire roared on, up the far wall and on to the plain beyond.

In the coulée, drifting plumes rose from smoking buffalo chips, and clumps of buckbrush crackled fitfully. A great wave of stinking smoke rolled from the buffalo run, where tons of bones smouldered sickeningly. But Ted did not notice. He had crawled to the edge of the water, where he tried to stand; but the shock of his fall and the smoke in his lungs made his head whirl, and bright lights flashed all around. He lay still for a moment, looking through the smoke toward the west; and as the haze thinned he caught

sight of the mountains—the friendly hills that had sheltered him for three years and more. They seemed like a
haven to him now.

"Mountains!" he croaked, and the sound of his voice
startled him; "I must—get—to—the mountains."

Weakly he tried to crawl; but then a wave of darkness
rolled over him and he knew nothing more.

On the second day after Ted's departure, René Corteau
called his friend from the cabin.

"Jeem, w'at you t'eenk of dat?" He pointed to the south-
east, where a yellowish cloud was forming.

"Huh! Looks like dust or smoke," muttered James.
"Come on up to the top of the bank and we'll have a good
look."

They climbed on their horses and headed up the south
bank. There they paused to watch in horror as the whole
horizon was hidden by the billowing smoke.

"Great Scott!" cried James. "The whole prairie is on
fire! Look, it goes right up to the foothills. Ted's out in
that, René. I wonder if he's all right?"

"Don' you worry none about dat fellow. He's know
pretty good how to look after heemself, you bet."

René tried to keep James from thinking of the possible
danger, but he could not hide the worry in his own voice as
they looked far to the south toward the line of fire. The
flames could not yet be seen, but the smoke rolled up along
a twenty-mile front, unhindered by wet or bare ground,
nourished by the long tangle of dry grass, driven by the
relentless wind. They knew that it could only be a matter

of hours before the fire reached the place where they stood, and right to the homestead, if something did not happen to stop it soon. They realized that they must at least try to save the buildings and the trees of the valley.

A back-fire was one way, and they tried it. They tied bundles of sticks together to make torches, and lit small fires around the house. When the little fires had got started, they put them out, and lit others between the burned spots, letting the grass burn upwind slowly and under control. Little by little they managed to burn off most of the grass around the yard and up onto the bench. This circle of burned grass would keep the flames away from their cabin unless the wind was strong enough to jump the clearing. If such a thing happened, they could do nothing.

"René," James spoke slowly, after thinking for a while, "I can see no point in our staying here. We can't hope to do more to fight the fire than we have done, and we can't possibly ride into that wall of flame to look for Ted."

He bowed his head and sighed, and for the next few minutes he said nothing; but Corteau knew that he was praying, and closed his eyes to say a prayer of his own. Then James raised his head.

"Come, René," he said wearily. "Let us ride out."

"Oui, Jeem. I'm come. But I'm bet you dat Ted, he's come too."

"Pray God he will, René. We can only hope for it."

They stopped only long enough to load their packs, and set out immediately for the crossing. In silence they walked the horses along the trail through the woods, splashed across the river, and climbed the north bank. The cloud was thickening fast, and they could smell the burning grass.

They had not gone five miles, though, when the first

drops of rain fell. Both men looked at the sky, and at each other, and halted. The sky was black above them, blotting out the yellow of smoke. The splashes fell all around them in the dry grass, and soon their clothes were damp.

Then the heavens opened. Through the glistening slant of the rain there fluttered a feathery white flake, and more, until the air was filled with large, ghostly flakes of snow. The first snowfall of winter had started, though it melted as soon as it touched the ground. Suddenly the soaked men realized that the weather had turned colder.

James and René sat their horses in silence, watching more clouds roll in from the west. The smoke was thinning now, all along the front, and they could see great clouds of it whipped high into the air as the wind suddenly changed direction.

"We can't leave now, without trying," burst out James, and René followed as the man turned his pony back toward the river. Side by side they rode through the water again, across the flat bottomlands of the valley floor, and up the south bank, while the smell of burned grass filled the air. Though the snow swirled all around them, they kept on through the storm. Soon they could hardly see the ground in front of them, but still they pushed onward, heads bowed before the fury of the blizzard.

Suddenly they were on the edge of a coulée, and when they went down the steep bank, they found themselves at the edge of a shallow marsh. They turned their horses to ride around the water, though they had a hard time telling just where the edge of the water was, for the surface was covered with ashes. Once across the soggy ground, they smelled the awful stench of the buffalo carcasses.

Even through the screen of snow they could see the cloud

of smoke and steam which rose from the huge pile of bones, and in the comparative silence of the valley the hiss of water on hot ashes was loud. Above them the storm swept on, blinding and white, and hiding all sight across the prairie.

"I guess it's no use, René." James drew his mount away from the bones, heading back across the coulée. "I don't suppose we could get very far in this storm, and we have no idea where the boy is. But let's just have a look around this slough. He might have been able to reach it in time." They walked their horses slowly along the edge of the marsh, eyes wide in hope that they might spot a still form. All around the marsh they rode, stepping the ponies around the swollen bodies of animal victims, gently speaking to them when they shied away from some dead form. In a few minutes they were back where they started. They sat for a moment longer, wondering, then Corteau said reassuringly:

"Jeem, Jeem, my ol' fren', don' you worry. Dat Ted, he's not gone be lost very long time. He's got to some place w'ere he be safe, I'm bet yo'. Ol' Corteau, he's tell you dat boy gone be all right." But the two of them made a sorrowful pair as they wearily rode back to the cabin at Spitzee. All thought of return to Edmonton was gone from MacDonnell's mind now.

"We must stay here, René. Just in case he does come back. He may be hurt, you know, and then he'll need us. I can't leave him now."

"Dat's plenty good t'eeng, I'm t'eenk, Jeem. But what yo' pretty wife gone t'eenk w'en yo' bot' don' come home dis winter. She's gone be pretty sad, I'm bet yo?" Corteau looked deep into his friend's eyes, and MacDonnell suddenly remembered his wife back at Edmonton.

"I must stay here and wait for Ted!" he snapped. "René, will you ride back to the fort and tell her what is happening? Don't tell her the boy may be dead, just say that he's out hunting and I'm waiting here for him. Tell her that if he does not come soon, I'll come back to see her every few weeks. Tell her to have patience, René, and trust me. You ought to be able to ride to the fort in a week, and get back here before the real winter hits." He looked hopefully at the Canadian. "Can't you?"

"Oui, mon ami. Ol' Corteau can do anyt'eeng hees fren' want heem to do. I'm gone right now, me, an' I be back in nine, ten day, I bet yo'. By gar, I'm ride so fas' you t'eenk I'm on fire, eh?" So saying, he dug his heels into the pony's ribs and headed away to the north.

James dismounted, unsaddled his horse, and turned it into the new log corral. Then he unlatched the cabin door and went inside to unpack his saddlebags.

Chapter Nineteen

WHITE CALF watched the women of his family as they stretched the fresh hides of deer and elk across wooden frames. When they were cured, some would be used with the hair on to make clothing for the coming winter, while others, scraped bare, would go to make the covering of a new tepee. The band had grown larger in the past few years, as other bands joined it for protection and survival; and White Calf's family had grown larger, also.

Each winter they had made the long trip into the hills, which offered protection from the winter's fury and provided plenty of food and fuel, while keeping the people away from the white men who caused other tribes to fight and kill their own brothers and fathers. Now they were busy setting up their permanent winter camp.

For the past few days they had noticed the grey-blue haze far to the eastward, and they knew that grass was burning. They thought nothing of it, for it happened often during the dry summers. Sometimes it started from some careless fire-builder, sometimes it was done purposely, for where the grass was burned, it grew back greener and better the next year, and the roving herds of buffalo would be attracted to the area.

White Calf looked for a moment at the sun, which hung near midday, and knew that it was almost time for him to climb the rock to take the place of Skinned Horse, who had been on lookout since dawn. As he made his way up the rough slope of the hill, the young man looked out over the plain, toward the haze of smoke, and saw the yellow and grey pall rise high in the air. He greeted his friend Skinned Horse, and sat on a ledge facing the trail from the east.

As the minutes passed he began to notice a stronger smell of fire, and stood up and sniffed carefully. There was no mistaking the odour of burning grass. The fire was coming near, nearer than fire had ever come to these hills, and as he watched, the wind began to freshen. He strained his eyes over the distance, but in the bright sunlight there was little to be seen save the long cloud on the horizon. For several hours he sat there, alone and watchful, till the day began to darken, partly from the coming night, partly from the smoke that now filled the sky all around him and nearly hid the sun.

He heard the rattle of loose stones from below and the soft call of one of his friends. The other Indian joined him and together they looked out over the miles to where the grass flamed in sudden flashes and bursts as vagrant winds caught it. The front of the fire was still several miles away, but the band was preparing to move out, unless something stopped the fire.

That something happened a short while later. First the wind fell until there was hardly a breath of air moving; then, very gently at first but with swiftly increasing violence, came the rain. It seemed like one of those sudden mountain squalls that sweep down the valleys and pass almost before one knows they have been; but this time the rain did not pass quickly. Instead, the youths on the cliff top felt the sudden change in temperature as the wind shifted to the northwest. Almost magically the rain began to change from silver to white, and great soft snowflakes landed on the warm rocks around them. The snow melted when it touched, but it fell heavily and silently, blotting out all view from where they sat. The flickering fires on the plains were hidden by the blanket, and only the smell of burning wood told them that their own camp still lay in the valley below.

The snow began to fall faster then, and with a rising wind it turned into a real blizzard, which made the lads huddle down behind the rocks, lying close so that the heat from the stones would give them some comfort from the chill wind that began to blow in gusts across the hilltops. Below them they heard the snap of tent covers flying in the wind and knew that their people would be out with strong stakes and big rocks to fasten the edges firmly. For perhaps an hour they lay where they were, talking softly to each other beneath the roar of the storm, and gradually the wind died, the snow stopped, and they were able once again to look out over the country.

Night had almost come now, and in the cool, moist evening air after the storm had passed, they saw that the prairie fire had been stopped. Clouds of steam and smoke boiled up from the brush slopes, and then died out, leaving a few patches smouldering fitfully, to die soon from want of dry fuel. When White Calf climbed back down to the camp, stars were bright and peaceful once again. The camp settled down for the night, trusting in the lone sentry who squatted in his blanket on the hilltop.

The next morning brought food, more food than White Calf had ever seen; for with the coming of daylight came the flood of refugees from the fire. For miles on all sides the grass had been destroyed, and all the creatures that had lived on the prairie now sought shelter and food in the hill country. They overran the bordering hills—deer, antelope, elk and even buffalo. Coyotes, rabbits, wolves and birds of every kind came flooding into the valleys.

Though the Indians were soon filled with good meat, they could not neglect this opportunity to lay in a supply for the winter. The women began to arrange the materials for the making of pemmican, building drying racks for the meat, gathering large quantities of dried berries, and sewing the many buckskin bags that would be needed to hold the supplies. While the squaws went about their work, the men took up their bows and spears and rode out toward the fire area in the hope of finding some larger game, perhaps a small herd of buffalo, or even antelope.

Skins and robes were always welcome, even in times of plenty, for any extra could be traded to the white men for powder and knives and other things. Anything they managed to get would be valuable, they knew, and the young men and boys went out eagerly.

The day was quiet—too quiet, for many of the common wild sounds were still; the birds and insects were gone. As the party approached the burned land, they came upon many carcasses of animals that had survived the actual fire but died of burns or injuries. From any they thought worth the trouble, they stripped the pelt, hoping it would go to make tent covers or clothing. Finally they arrived at the edge of the grass, and even after two days of fresh winds the air was still heavy with the scent of burned hay.

Far out over the black plain they could see the naked grey shape of a great rock. It was not so large as the Okotoks, but the huge cave inside had been used for centuries as a shelter. The hunters headed for the rock, hoping to be able to see some sign of life from the top of the boulder.

The rock lay alone and silent in the middle of the burn. The party approached it cautiously, for often they had trapped animals in the cave. They left their horses some distance downwind and crept stealthily on foot to the great stone shell. When the rock was completely surrounded so that any possible victim could not escape, they closed in. There was not much hope that there would be anything in the hole, but it was a game for the Indians. They advanced slowly. Nothing moved as they covered the entrance. Nothing moved as they stepped inside. Indeed, the form that lay on the ground could not move, for Ted was far too weak to care who had trapped him.

"*Sukanabi!*" cried White Calf, and in a moment the white boy was tenderly being cared for, as one Indian held his head up, and another gave him a sip from a waterskin. Ted was far from dead, and even managed to murmur: "White Calf—been looking all over for you for a long while——" before he was offered a little dried meat and fat.

With the tiny bit of food inside him, Ted decided it was worth while to live, and tried to help as the Indians rolled him gently onto the travois and tied him there in a cocoon of fresh, soft hides. White Calf walked beside his friend, leading his pony, doing his best to show how happy he was to have his friend with him again. Ted fell asleep to the rocking and bumping and swaying of the travois, his stomach feeling the dull ache of hunger that his mouthful of food had aroused.

He did not know when they reached the camp, nor did he hear the cries of welcome when they saw him, cries quickly stilled lest his sleep be disturbed. He woke as they carried him into a large tent, and he was served a hot stew of rabbit and some kind of greens, and with his stomach full for the first time in days, his burns soothed with grease, he fell asleep again.

The Stony women tended him faithfully, and while he rested, the men went on with their hunt. And as he lay there, weak and sore from his burns and cuts, he lived again the painful trip from the swamp to the rock. For hour after hour he had crawled toward the mountains, knowing nothing of time, feeling little save the compulsion that drove him on toward the west. He remembered little of the actual journey, nor did he know for sure how he had crossed the many streams and coulées on the way. But at last he was safe with his friends. He stopped thinking and slept.

The Stonies had never seen so much game as they ran down during the next few days. They gorged themselves on the choicest parts; then they turned to the work of drying and preserving meat for the winter. While some of the women spent all day on the hillsides picking the few withered berries that the birds had missed, and digging up large piles of roots and herbs, others sliced the meat into long, thin strips and hung it across the drying racks set up over the low, wide fires.

When the meat had dried enough, it was ground to powder and mixed well with melted fat. Berries and some kinds of roots were then added, and the whole mixture packed tightly into the skin bags, and sewn up with sinews. These bags would keep for years, and the food in them could be eaten as it was, or roasted, fried, boiled or baked. The full bags were stacked in one small tent, and they laid up enough to carry the whole band through the winter if the meat supply should suddenly fail.

There was so much game in the hills by this time that the men grew tired of hunting every day. They saw the pile of bags the women had filled, and they saw the great quantity of meat that was on hand; so they forgot hunting for a while, and turned to other things. The days were warm after the first snow; and with a warm lodge and plenty of meat, with pemmican laid by, what more could an Indian want?

Chapter Twenty

TED lay quietly on his bed of skins, waiting till White Calf came back with something to eat. For the past two days, it seemed to him, he had done nothing but eat. He turned his head to peek through the door slit, and saw the bright autumn sunlight streaming through the pines. For two days he had lain still, and he found that he could do so no longer. He rolled onto his side and pushed himself up with one arm. Gathering his feet under him, he stood slowly upright. The tepee began to spin around him, but he put one hand to a pole and the spinning stopped. Then he discovered that his feet would not obey him. With great effort he managed to move one foot ahead of the other with a sliding motion. When he put his weight on it, the tent started whirling again.

Another short step made him feel better. He moved closer to the door and the fresh morning air tasted clean and sweet as it blew in at the opening. Cautiously he held to the tent poles as he stuck his head outside. There was not a soul in sight. Somehow he managed to lift one leg high enough to step through the door hole, but he almost fell the rest of the way. It took several minutes to get both legs through the doorway, but finally he was outside, out in the bright sunshine, out in the brisk October air. The Indian camp lay quiet, but on the edge of the tented area he could hear a group of squaws talking as they skinned out the tails of the buffalo that had been shot on the hunt.

Before he could take even one step away from the tent, he heard his name called from some distance away, and in a moment came the sound of running feet, as White Calf dashed up.

"Sukanabi! What are you doing?" The Indian youth caught Ted's arm to steady him. "You cannot walk yet. You must stay in the tent until you are well again. A man does not starve one day and run races the next." But Ted would not return to his bed. He insisted that he be allowed to sit outside in the fresh air and sunshine, so his friend settled him against the tent wall and went to get the chunk of boiled buffalo hump he had been seeking. Ted raised his eyes along the grey wall of the cliff that rose above the camp, and at the top, barely visible even to his keen eyes, was the figure of the lookout, motionless against the sky. Surely, he thought, no enemy could surprise this camp.

The days that followed were slow ones for Ted. The burns healed, and little by little he grew healthy under the kind care of the Indians. Gradually his singed hair grew again, and his fits of coughing grew less severe. The plentiful supply of meat kept most of the camp busy curing and grinding and mixing pemmican, but each member of the band found time during the day to stop for a friendly chat. Within a week Ted was able to walk slowly around the camp watching the natives at their work. He smiled to himself as he saw the women cut up pieces of meat and place them in skin-lined holes in the ground. It seemed like hours before they had heated enough stones to boil the water in these crude pots, but Ted suddenly remembered that he had nothing else to do anyway. He was in no hurry. He recalled that it was this method of cooking that had given the Stonies their name, Assiniboine, or "the people who cook with hot stones".

"What a difference," he thought, "from the last time I camped around here! Then I did all my own hunting and butchering and cooking. Now I just sit around and do nothing, and get waited on hand and foot." It was rather nice, for a change, yet he felt somehow that he would be happier doing it himself.

The fall days were warm and sunny, and even though snow fell one evening, it was all gone by the next morning. It was on just such a day that Ted took his first ride. It felt good to straddle a pony again. He was riding a shaggy little mare, fat as a buffalo cow, and gentle as a rabbit. With White Calf beside him he rode out across the hills.

"White Calf," he said, turning to his friend as they loped along over the now thin grass, "when you found me I was in some kind of a cave, wasn't I?"

The Indian boy nodded. "Yes, my friend. You were in the magic cave."

"Magic cave?" Ted stared blankly, waiting for the other to explain.

"Yes, it is the cave of stories. For many years my people have hunted close by this cave. It is filled with many pictures made by the old ones." Ted knew that the "old ones" were the ancestors of the Indians, probably not of the same tribe or nation, but nevertheless the first people of the plains. But something seemed not quite right to Ted.

"But, White Calf, if it is a cave and is big enough to live in, where is it? It seemed to me that it was right out in the middle of the prairie."

"That is right. It *is* in the middle of the prairie. It is in a great rock which my fathers say the gods put there as a marker. That is why it is magic."

At these words Ted suddenly remembered the other big rock, the Okotoks, far to the north. Here were two huge stones, all by themselves in the plain. How had they come there, miles from the nearest mountains? Perhaps they were the tops of mountains that had become covered with earth. Perhaps they were new mountains, just forming. At that moment they came in sight of the rock.

It stuck up from the blackened prairie, and the huge hole in one side was black in the afternoon shadow. Very cautiously they approached, watching to see what animal might be within. They were disappointed, for nothing was in the cave but a dirty drift of unmelted snow. Ted walked into the cave without hesitating, but White Calf hung back, a little in awe of the mysterious place. After a moment he took courage and followed his friend.

Inside the cave was dark, but as their eyes became used to the gloom, Ted could see the far walls and the ceiling. It was on the ceiling that he saw the paintings first. Like the markings on the Okotoks, these appeared to be mostly straight lines; but soon he could make out figures with arms and legs, and circles and arrows, and in one spot there was a crude, partly spoiled figure that he knew was meant to be a buffalo. In other places there were drawings that looked as though they might be corrals, with figures inside.

Some of the drawings were strange to Ted, for he had seen nothing like them, even on the walls at Okotoks.

Ted and White Calf talked together about the signs they could recognize—the sign of war in Blackfoot, the sign of scouts, and the records of captured horses. When they could read no more of the pictures they turned to leave. Ted stepped out into the sunlight, blinking in the brightness, but before he could take another step he felt his arm grasped in a powerful grip and he was almost yanked off his feet as White Calf pulled him back into the cave.

"Wha—what's wrong?" Ted stammered, startled by his friend's action.

"Sukanabi, you are a white man, after all," scolded the Indian. "Indian never goes from night into day with his eyes closed. If a Blackfoot war party was outside, you could not see to fight them. You must learn to look and listen well before you go where you are not sure of safety."

Ted had shown his white blood when he stepped from the shelter without first looking in every direction and listening carefully—listening not so much for the beat of hooves or the fall of a foot, but for the change in the normal sounds of the prairies, the screams of hawks in the sky, the rustle and whine of insects, the passage of magpies. Few animals had yet ventured back onto the burned grasslands, but those that were there could tell him what he wanted to know. He peered cautiously from the gloom of the cave mouth, and White Calf grunted his approval, bright eyes also alert. Their ears and eyes told them that nothing was abroad to threaten their passage, so they walked to their horses and mounted.

When the rock was behind them and they headed back

toward the hills and the camp, White Calf turned across his pony and spoke:

"My father and my family are planning to hunt in the shining hills in a day's time." He pointed toward the glistening, snow-capped mountains. "Would my white brother join us? Or does he think he is not yet strong enough?" Ted thought for a minute or two, and replied:

"Well, I guess I'm about as well as I'll ever be, and what I need is some good exercise. I'd be mighty pleased to come with you."

"Good," smiled the Indian, and they kicked their ponies into a faster pace, making little puffs of black dust in the burned grass.

For another full day they loafed around camp, while the squaws finished packing pemmican, and on the final night before the hunt every man took time for a sweat bath. A dozen tiny lodges for this purpose had been set up in the camp, and White Calf's family used three that night, taking turns. Ted had not been in a sweat lodge since his first return to Edmonton, and was eager to climb into the low, skin-covered framework of sticks. He seated himself on the stones that lined the floor of the tent, and in a moment the flap opened and a smoking-hot stone rolled in. Upon this stone Ted poured a little of the water he had in a small bowl, and immediately the tent was filled with warm vapour. As each stone cooled, Ted rolled it outside, and it was replaced with a hot one. For half an hour he sat and enjoyed the luxury, and when it was time to leave, he did so with reluctance. But once outside, the fresh wind soon made him aware that he was alive, and he hurried into his clothes, feeling fit and ready for anything.

The morning dawned slowly, and it was cold. A band of grey clouds hid the sun and followed it all the way up into the sky, so that they left camp in near-darkness and dreary chill. Ted chose a new horse, a piebald mare much like his old horse that had been lost in the fire, and with a short lance for a weapon, he took his place in the long line of hunters that began to wind along the track between the hilltops.

They travelled all that day without sighting anything worth chasing, and that night camped near the top of a hill where a lookout could see all the country below, and where an attacking enemy would have to fight uphill. In the morning they ate quickly, without fire, for smoke would carry far in the clear air, as would the smell of burning wood. Animals as well as men might take notice.

They were climbing on their horses ready to ride when White Calf's father called out a loud command. Ted knew that something important was about to take place, but when he was called, he could not understand what was about to happen. He rode slowly toward the old Indian, watched silently and closely by all the hunters. He halted his pony several paces from Many Horses, waiting until he was spoken to. The leader of the band stared at him for a long time, without saying anything, and Ted gazed steadily into the old grey eyes. Then the Indian spoke clearly to him, so that all in the party might hear.

"Sukanabi, you are my son. You have lived with us for many days now, and when you first came to this country you wished to be our friend. Now you wish to hunt with us. You have been very near to death and we have made you well. And in this task of making you well we have forgotten something which is very important to you." Ted could see the corners of the old man's mouth twitching a little, as though he were suppressing a smile. Then he noticed that smiles were on the faces of many of the others, and the mystery deepened.

Many Horses made a motion with his hand, and White Calf rode to his side, carrying something across his knees. Ted gasped. He recognized the fringed and worn gun case he had made years past, when he had lived in the mountains. It was his old long rifle! He could say nothing when it was handed to him. He could only stare at it in wonder, and then at the friends around him.

"How——?" He could not finish. But White Calf answered his unspoken question.

"You wonder how we have come to have your rifle, Sukanabi? You left it in a tepee near the crossing by the big stone called Okotoks. It was standing by the door. Our warriors found it there."

"*Your* warriors!" exclaimed Ted, not believing his ears.

"Yes," White Calf said gently. "We made a raid on the Blackfoot camp to get more horses. When we found your rifle but not you, we thought you had been killed by the Blackfeet. We were very sad and very angry with the Blackfeet. We killed some of them and drove them from the camp. We kept your rifle because it held your spirit. I have kept it loaded all the time. Your rifle is strong hunter's medicine. We give it back to you."

At a loss for words, Ted stared at the silent men around him. "Why—White Calf—I was in the tepee when you came. I heard the fighting and went out under the back of the tent. Later I came back to get the rifle, but your men had already taken it. I thought they might be Crees or some other enemy, and I ran far away. I stayed all winter in the mountains. If I had only known it was you who had come——"

"Yes, my friend, it is too bad that you were forced to go to the great hills in wintertime. But these things happen often in our lives on the prairies."

They did not care too much about the amount of game they got on this hunt, for they had food aplenty back at the camp, and these trips were to get fresh meat, so that their store of pemmican need not be used unless necessary. They rode far into the hills, searching for game that would be worth killing; and they rode in single file, each man on the lookout for signs of life.

But the game that had been so abundant had now largely disappeared. Where only a short time ago the grass had been high and thick, now it was cropped to the bare ground. The animals, driven into the hills in such unprecedented numbers, had grazed off the whole supply in that district. Even the low branches of the trees had been stripped of bark and leaves. Very little wild life was left.

They rode on toward the mountains, for far from the fire they must find plenty of game. As they rode over a hill and started down into the next canyon, one of the leaders pointed ahead and then held up a warning hand. The file stopped, waiting. Those at the back of the line could hardly see what was sighted; but as they sat, an elk left a clump of trees and started across the valley. It walked slowly toward them, head up, watchful; but they were still too far for it to see them clearly. Not a man moved, not a horse moved. Ted waited, itching to line up on a target again. A low grunt passed down the line from man to man as the leaders asked for any man who thought he might bring down the animal at this range, for it was a long shot. Ted looked hopefully at his friends, and as the question reached him, he hesitated only a moment before nodding.

Glancing along the line of waiting men, Ted could read the expressions of approval in their eyes. He took the rifle from the case, thrilling to the trust and honour they had given him. With the touch of the master he looked to priming, drew back the hammer, and rested his arms a moment on the horse's back. Then, sitting bolt upright on his pony, he raised the gun. The hunters in front moved out of the way, and Ted found his sights lined directly on the slowly moving elk.

It was nearly half a mile away, and the ball of the front sight almost covered it. Ted steadied the gun, freezing into rock-like immobility; then he stopped breathing and squeezed the trigger. The rifle had been well loaded, and a good round ball sped to its mark. After the blast of the shot there came not a sound or move from any of the hunters as they stared breathlessly at the target. It seemed like an hour before Ted saw the animal sink slowly to its knees, then collapse on its side. Then came the whoops and screams of triumph from a score of native throats. Relieved and happy, Ted grinned at White Calf.

"Looks like that was a pretty well set ball and charge you put in this gun," he said.

"Sukanabi!" laughed White Calf. "Remember, you taught me how to shoot with this rifle. I loaded it as you would yourself, and I knew that you would not miss." A gruff voice broke upon them.

"The white Stony is the greatest hunter of the plains, and of all the world," said Many Horses, laying a fond hand on Ted's shoulder. "We knew that the man who wears this"—he pointed to the bear-claw necklace—"was a brave warrior, and now we know that he is also a skilful hunter. I am honoured that he has chosen to ride with my band." And so saying, the head of the family took Ted's hand in his own, pressed it tight for a moment, then turned his pony away up the trail, toward the slain elk.

Chapter Twenty-one

T HE three days of hunting passed quickly, for the men
were not worrying about the amount of food they got.
The large supplies in their camp were nearly enough to do
all winter, and most of all they wanted more skins for
clothing and shelter against the winter cold.

Judging from the piles of elk hides and deerskins, as well
as buffalo robes, that were piled back in the camp, it looked
to Ted as though the Stonies would have a very comfortable winter indeed. And the hunt would bring many more
hides. Ted used his long rifle to good advantage, happy to
have it in his hands again, glad to be able to use it to help
his Stony friends. They spent nearly three days in the
hills, and then turned back toward their camp. Not a man
among them was unhappy, and the younger men laughed
and sang much of the time.

They thought of the great supply of food that was laid
up at their camp, and of the pile of furs that would keep

them warm in the cold weather. They pictured the snug camp, in its sheltered place under a good lookout point, with plenty of wood for their fires, and water aplenty for drinking and bathing. It seemed that it might be a good winter, and they looked forward to it with full hearts.

Then they came within earshot of the camp, and even at that distance the wail of the women carried to them clearly. They sped up their pace, cantering into the village to be greeted with howls of lamentation. Then the sad news was told them. On the day after the hunters had gone out of the camp, it had happened. Very early that morning, not long before daybreak, the women and old men had been awakened by a great noise from the direction of the prairies, and when they rushed out to see what was happening, they discovered that a huge pack of wolves was dashing toward them. There was not a gun in the camp. They were armed only with bows and spears.

Unable to stop the wolves, the people ran terrified to the hillside, where they climbed the cliff out of reach of the beasts, and watched in anger and horror as the hunger-maddened pack raced through the camp, tearing at the tepees, scattering the fires and destroying all the clothing they could find in their efforts to find food. Then they came to the tepee that held the supply of meat and pemmican.

In half an hour the band's entire supply of food was either eaten or dragged away by the ravenous animals. The horses left in camp were stampeded, and those that were not killed broke through the corral ropes and raced away into the hills. When they had finished the meat and the dead horses, the wolves grew quiet and soon began to break up into small groups, which disappeared into the trees, and soon the camp was empty again. When the last beast disappeared, the people came down from the rocks, wailing and crying, for they knew what would come of this misfortune.

The whole camp was wrecked. Some of the tepees were still standing, but the skin coverings had been slashed to ribbons by the teeth of the wolves; and of the meat tent, not so much as a tuft of hair remained. They had eaten meat, skins, lashings, and all but the bare poles. For another whole day and night the women had sat around their ruined camp, fixing what they could, repairing what was possible, and all the while wailing their curious chant. The old men simply sat and stared at the scene with bleak eyes, for they knew that many of them would die of starvation and cold before another spring. In the midst of the confusion and misery the hunters returned.

Ted was shocked at the sight of the camp. What had been a neat and orderly village, looked like the aftermath of a great storm. But he joined the rest of the Indians in trying to right the damage, helping the squaws erect the fallen tents, sew together the torn coverings, and even patch the great holes that had been eaten out of the skins.

The destroyed meat supply could not be replaced. The whole tribe knew that they faced a hungry winter, and immediately a band of hunters was sent out to find food. The whole company of women and children spread out over the woods and fields, moving slowly across the uneven ground, digging and gathering roots and plants, picking every withered and dry berry, bagging all the small game that lived in the grass and would make a mouthful. Though they were not yet hungry, a few days would see the beginning of hardships. The snow would soon come, and then they would be hard put to live.

Ted volunteered to hunt, and managed to bag a large number of grouse and rabbits, for these animals could live on the short grass that was left in the area. Even a few wandering deer were to be had. The first snow fell four days after the raid of the wolves, and every hide and skin was needed to keep out the cold that began to settle over the mountains. Each tepee had its own fire, built in the centre of the tent, and the smoke rose through the hole at the top, through the smoke flaps. All around the lower part of the tents there hung an inside curtain of deer hide, to keep in the heat of the fire, and with their supply of furs they were able to stay quite comfortable. Their clothes were in very good condition, all except for moccasins, and new ones were made by the busy women.

Ted went out with the men to help build traps and set up snares for wandering rabbits and other small game. The Indians pinned much faith on the traps, for it was a quiet and simple method; but Ted chose to follow his game, and he often came across the trail of elk and deer, which he followed until he was close enough to drop the animals with single shots. And each time he brought back one of the larger animals, the band had plenty to eat. But the occasions grew rare, and he had to hunt farther and harder. He found that no matter how carefully he looked and listened, his Indian friends could spot the game more quickly and easily. Where Ted might see one deer, the Indians could see many, and he became quite disgusted with himself.

The tracks in the woods were few and far between by this time, and again Ted marvelled at the ability of his native partners to see deer or other game, or to know where to find them. He might be travelling with others, perhaps White Calf, when all of a sudden one of the Indians would stop. That was the signal for the party to halt, freeze in their tracks, look and listen. It meant that the man had seen, smelled or heard something.

Ted would sniff the air, strain his ears, look until his eyes popped out, but he could detect nothing. Then the Indian would silently point to some dense part of the forest, and after watching for a few minutes Ted would see the elk standing there, watching them, placidly eating the bark off a tree. If he was able, he would shoot it. But more often than not he could not get a clear shot at it, and the animal would wander into deeper woods before he could get a sight on it. Then it became a game of chase. They would plough through the snow in pursuit, ending when the elk could no longer buck the drifts in the trees and was overtaken, or when the animal reached a clear area and vanished over the hill. Then the hunters could not take time to follow, for in chasing one they might pass up others close by.

Usually Ted went with other hunters when they searched for game, but sometimes he found himself alone. On such occasions he would venture into parts of the hills where he had never been before, and sometimes was able to bring back meat. But no matter how much they killed, or how hard they hunted, the food supply gradually dwindled, and the hunters had more and more difficulty making kills within the area. They began to come back empty-handed. Then the situation became serious. There were over a hundred souls in the camp, counting children, and soon they would have to eat the horses, even as the Blackfeet had done the year before.

But in the Stony camp there was no sound of complaint. When one family went hungry, all were hungry. When one hunter returned with a kill, it was shared among the whole camp, with every family expecting and taking its share. Ted had no family save his adopted one, that of White Calf, and his meat was divided among all the others so that a deer did not last long, and a few birds gave hardly a mouthful to each; yet they took what was theirs and said nothing.

Yet each day they grew hungrier, and Ted could tell how desperate they were becoming by the way they looked at the horses. There were only the horses that had been taken by the party that had gone on the hunt, and they were the most precious possessions of the tribe. They could not be sacrificed if other food could possibly be had.

The first weeks of real winter were very cold, for snow fell early and the frost bit deeply into the tents. Had it not been for the tepee linings, the fires could not have kept out the icy air. The iron of spear points glistened like jewels, and guns were too cold to hold with bare hands. During these days the game disappeared from around the camp until there was not so much as a magpie in the whole country, and the women went out to the nearby woods to look for the tiny tracks of mice that would tell them where the nest might be. Soon there was nothing left to kill and nothing to eat but the dogs and horses.

Ted watched with pity as the last of the dogs was cooked, but he ate his share eagerly. When the dogs were gone, they started on the horses. First, as the Blackfeet had done, they killed only the oldest and poorest, hoping that each day would bring other meat for their pots. One horse was slaughtered each day and shared among the whole village. Twenty-three horses lasted just twenty-three days. When the last was gone, they started on leather.

Old moccasins, worn or torn, were boiled day and night, and chewed and sucked to take out the salt and what juice might be had. The leather was eaten when the people became hungry enough. They had plenty of skins, to be sure, and they had plenty of wood for the fires. But other meat must be had. Ted and White Calf had vowed to each other to do their best to keep the people alive through the winter, but it began to look like an impossible task.

One day a hunter did not return. The men who were able went out to find him, but they crawled back without him. And soon another man disappeared into the white hills and was lost. One by one the old hunters failed to come back, and in a few weeks only a score of young men remained in the village. Ted and White Calf spent much time trying to find the lost men, but their efforts were in vain, for the drifting snows hid all sign of tracks and bodies, and a starving man lost in the hill country for more than a day or two in winter had no hope of being rescued. Ted sadly noted the thinning ranks of his friends. All the happiness was gone from him now. He pledged himself to serve the camp.

There was not a tent in the camp that did not have an empty space, and every woman wailed her lament. The children were silent, for they had not the strength to make sounds, and their movements were restricted to helping with the daily chores—what there were without cooking or sewing or tanning.

Ted left the camp. He said nothing to anyone, not

even to White Calf; he simply took his gun and bag and
went out into the winter day. He was not running away.
He was searching for another place to camp, one where
they might take what was left of the band and find better
hunting. He headed west, into the mountains, knowing
that there he would find deeper snow and colder winds,
but there was the chance that on the windswept hillsides
there might be elk grazing on the exposed grass, or perhaps
sheep or goats.

For two or three hours he walked, searching for tracks
that would lead him to meat. He thought of the "meat
mine" that Jake pretended to have discovered at Edmonton, and wished it might come true here. When he came
to a bare rock on the hillside he stopped to rest. All the
strength seemed to have gone from him and the ache of
hunger now filled his whole body. The cramps were worst
when he stopped. Gasping for breath, blowing great
clouds of vapour on the frosty air, he fought to clear his
head of the ringing in it.

The sun was very bright, and perhaps that was what
made him notice the little cloud of steam. It was not steam
from his own breath; it seemed to come from a tiny crack
in the rock under him. Another hot spring, he told himself,
and cocked an ear to try to pick up the bubbling music of
the stream that lay below.

But this stream did not bubble. It made a strange sound,
and Ted could not at first identify it. It seemed to come in
long, low whistles, or gasps, and he pictured in his mind
his friend, Corteau, flat on his back in his blankets, breathing loudly and steadily. It sounded just like a man sleeping.
Then Ted knew what it was.

Although he had lived in the hills for three or four years,

he had never come upon a hibernating bear; but he had heard of them, and was quite certain that that was what it must be. He remembered the men telling him how a bear would find a snug hole and crawl into it, to sleep all winter long. The beast's warm breath would usually melt a small hole in the snow that covered its lair. Ted sat there for a few moments, trying to decide what to do. Then he knew that there was only one sensible course—he must get help.

So back to the camp he went, retracing his steps as fast as he could. His great yell brought startled faces poking from the lodges. Then he told what he had found, and a cheer of joy went through the snow-bound tents. They gathered all the men together, but found that only three were fit to make the trip. They had to form some kind of plan that would not fail. Each man chose a spear, and one took a bow and arrows. They knew that if a gun were used, the noise would frighten away any other game that happened to be near, and they did not want to take that chance. Spears were silent. Dressed warmly against the hike, the four young men set out to find the sleeping bear.

Ted's trail was almost covered by the time they started, but the crust had been broken and made fairly easy going through the woods. Ted led them as quickly as possible to his discovery, but when they finally reached the place, he was exhausted. He fell on the snow and lay still, and the Indians left him there while they went about digging out the bear. Ted lay resting and watching them. They had done this before, he thought. They stuck their spears, point up, in a snowbank close to hand, and all three drew knives and started cutting away the hard snow beside the breathing hole. They worked without talking, and their weak condition made them slow, for they tired easily and had to stop to rest often.

By cutting down the snow bank they cleared a hole right into the dark den. From where Ted lay he could see nothing, so he got to his feet and went over. By this time the den was wide open, and proved to be nothing more than a crevice between two rocks, but the bear had settled himself there and even the working of the Indians did not disturb him. They cleared the remaining snow from around the hole, and Ted caught his first glimpse of the bear. It was a fat brute, with a heavy coat that would warm some lodge in a little while. The Indians laid aside their knives and motioned to Ted to grasp a spear, and they did likewise.

Each man took up a weapon, and the one with the bow then took out an arrow and notched it. They stood close around, spears poised almost against the bear's side, as the bowman raised and aimed his weapon and bent it. The shaft whirred from the string and sank feather-deep into the brown form, directly behind the shoulder. Instantly the spears touched the hide, ready to plunge, but they were not needed. The bear gave only a snort and stopped snoring. The arrow had pierced its heart.

They reached for the animal's forepaws to drag it out. The beast was so large and heavy that it took all the combined strength of the four men even to lift it enough to allow one man to crawl in beside the body and start to skin one hind leg. While he did this, another Indian built a pile of sticks and shredded bark, and Ted struck his flint to the back of his knife and the spark soon set the fire blazing, and the snow around it turned black and melted.

By the time the fire was burning well, the youth had cut

off the leg of the bear and handed it out, and in minutes slices of the meat were toasting on the points of four knives. They ate as much as they were able, licking their fingers afterward, for the bear was still fat from his summer of feasting. Then the four young men sat back to plan their next move.

Weak as they were, they could not hope to pack all the meat back to the camp, at least not for a few days, and every day counted when their people were starving. They decided that two would stay with the carcass and guard it, while the other two would take a small amount of the meat back to the camp so that each person would have at least a little food. Then they would bring help to carry the rest of the meat. One bear would not last them very long, even if they rationed it, but at least it would give them the strength they needed to move to another hunting ground.

Ted chose to stay, for he was very tired and stiff from two trips through the snow; and White Calf, who had come with him, stayed also. That night the two friends crept into the opened bear den, and partly closed it with snow blocks. Snuggling close to the thick fur of the dead beast, they were warm enough to sleep.

A shout woke them next day, and they crept out of the hole to see six Indians trudging toward them. Together the eight men managed to load the carcass onto a rude sled they made, and pulled it back to the village. They were met by the whole camp, crying and laughing in their joy at the prospect of the feast. Feast it was, too, for they ate until they could hardly walk, and some who had been close to death could not hold their food and were very sick. But they were given drinks of tea made from bark and leaves, and that evening were well again and able to eat as much as the next man.

For the first time in a month the band had full bellies, and now the older heads sat in conference to decide on the moving of the camp. To the west, they agreed, for where there was one bear there might be more, and perhaps much other game. They passed a pipe of tobacco and the decision was approved by all the council.

Chapter Twenty-two

THE move began early the next day, for to wait any
longer would have meant sure death. They could not
stay where there was no food. Men, women and children
bundled themselves warmly against the bitter wind and,
led by their chief, they made their way slowly into the
hills, seeking higher ground swept clear by the wind.
Almost from the start, it seemed, their luck changed for
the better. Before they had gone five miles they came upon
tracks. Both small game and large game had passed this
spot. It was White Calf who first spotted the prints, and
Ted was close beside him.

"See, white brother!" the Indian lad said to Ted. "See
how slowly he walks." They bent to inspect a trail of very
fresh elk tracks. "He cannot be far from us now. We must
be quiet and perhaps we shall see him."

"Yes, I have read the tracks," replied Ted. He squatted
beside the new trail. Very gently he touched the edges of

the broken snow with his finger tips. "The snow is dry, and the edges are still soft." Ted knew that if the track was more than a few minutes old it would be harder to the touch, for the surface of the snow would have crusted.

"We must hurry," said White Calf. "But he is close. Be silent."

They moved ahead of the other people, following the trail closely. The tracks were evenly spaced, Ted noted, showing long trails where each hoof had dragged. His experience in the woods told him that White Calf was right. The elk was only walking, for when going slowly, the animal did not lift its feet high, and the dragging marks resulted. Also, the closeness of the prints, the evenness of the spacing bore this out. If the elk had been running the prints would have been bunched together into clusters as he leaped in great strides, landing with feet together. His hooves would punch sharp holes in the snow where they landed, and make a short trail in front as they came out again. Also, his leaps would have been perhaps ten feet from print to print, in a direct line, not wandering in zigzag formation as these were.

Swiftly the two young hunters followed the tracks, and before long they knew they were close to their quarry.

"Wait, Sukanabi!" The Indian halted and listened. "He is starting to go faster. He is starting to run. He has scented or heard us."

"Well then, let's not waste time. Let's get to him before he gets away."

"It would be no good. We could never outrun him in the woods where there is little snow. Come, let us go this way." So saying, White Calf left the track to start out through the snow, moving in a direction away from where the tracks led.

"Where are you going? What are you doing?" called Ted, surprised.

"Sh-h-h-h! Make no sound," cautioned the Indian. He led on a few feet farther before he explained. "When he is being followed, an elk or deer will nearly always make a large circle and double back on his own trail so that the pursuers will be confused. He is making a circle to the right, for the tracks lead slightly that way. We will go a little way into the wood and wait for him to come back to us."

After a few minutes White Calf held up his hand and they halted, crouching in silence behind a fallen tree. Ted cocked his rifle and rested it on the trunk. They listened with all their power of hearing, and in a little while caught the faint sound of steps. Ted could see some distance through the trees, and far away he spotted the tawny form of the elk. White Calf saw it too, and they held their breath and waited. But the elk had chosen another path to follow, and it began to wander away from them.

Like a flash Ted slipped down lower in the snow, rolled over on his back, and pulled out his ramrod. With all the speed he could manage he drew the ball from the barrel and poured in another charge of powder, then rammed the ball home again and stuck the rod upright in the snow beside him. His rifle was double-charged now. It would deliver a kick that would shame a mule, he knew; but the range was too great for a single load. As he levelled the gun again, he heard his friend say:

"Hurry, Sukanabi—he is almost too far. Make a good sight, and I will stop him. When he stops you must shoot."

"Right!" grunted Ted softly, and lined up on the neck of the elk, which was moving farther away with each step. He had hardly taken his aim when a shrill whistle cut through the forest. Instantly the elk froze, ears up and swivelling to catch any further sound. On that instant Ted squeezed the trigger. The roar of the rifle echoed back and forth across the still countryside; and even before he heard it, Ted felt the weapon leap in his hands. It tore loose from his grip and smashed against his shoulder, and he tumbled backward into the snow.

His shoulder was numb and his ears rang; and when he struggled to sit up, the world was filled with the thunder of falling snow as it slid from the branches of every tree nearby. The powdery snow thudded all around him, almost burying him before he could get to his feet. He looked wildly around for his rifle, and for White Calf. The Indian was, like himself, nearly covered with snow, but he held up the rifle with one arm to keep it from being lost in the pile. Somehow he had managed to get it before it was covered.

They looked at each other for the length of a blink, and burst into loud laughter. As they made their way toward the place where the elk had been, they were still laughing. And when they stumbled over the nearly buried body of the animal, they could hardly believe their luck.

The elk was thin and tough, but when it was carried back to the waiting Indians, it was welcomed as though it were the tenderest buffalo. Once again they filled themselves, and since they could not walk farther that day, made camp for the night.

For nearly another week they went on, over hills and through valleys, looking for some place to live, some spot where water and firewood and game were plentiful. On the evening of the sixth day of their trip one of the scouts came running into camp, out of breath and sweating like a man in a sweat lodge. He had sighted an elk yard.

"Elk yard" was not exactly the term used by the Stonies; it was the nearest Ted could come to making sense of their words. The expression puzzled him, and he asked what it meant.

An elk yard, he was told, was like owning one's private herd. Sometimes in winter the animals would find a pasture where the grass was long under the snow, and could be reached by scraping. Gradually they would clear the snow away; and as more fell, and the herd stayed in the same place, a white wall would grow up around the pasture. After the elk had been in the field for some time the snow would become so deep all around that it formed a pen, trapping the animals. To kill one, all that was necessary was to wait on the high snowbank until an unwary beast wandered close, when it could be stabbed with a spear.

What better place to make camp? the Indians thought. Near the elk yard they trampled down the snow until it was firmly packed, then pitched their tepees. Snow blocks were piled high all around to make a windbreak, and the band settled down for the rest of the winter.

The snow in the woods had frozen over with a hard crust that allowed the people to walk on it without snowshoes, and it was easy to get all the meat they needed, for the elk could not get away from them. There was a lot of snow on the ground, and when the spring thaws came, the Indians would have to hurry to get out of the forest before they were caught in the soft slush that would hamper their movements. But that would not come for many weeks yet, and they did not worry about it, for they had shelter, food and skins, and plenty of wood for their fires. Once again they had survived the worst that Nature could do.

When the weather began to grow milder, when the top of the snow grew dirty and their moccasins sank into it, they knew that it was time to move again. Their first action was to slaughter part of the elk herd that was left in the yard. The meat was quickly dried and packed into skin bags, to form their reserve supply in case other fresh meat was not found before they reached a new camp. When they finally reached high ground, far above the normal run-off from the melting snows, where wind and sun had already bared the hills, they found a temporary camp site and set up their tents again.

With the coming of spring, the game increased so that they had plenty of food at all times, and now could turn to thoughts of how best to get back to the prairies. Horses were their chief topic of discussion, for without horses they were bound to one area. Ted could feel the excitement in the air, matching his own growing impatience to get out of the hills and make his way back to Spitzee. If his father and Corteau were still there, they would be waiting for him. He could not waste any more time, now that his friends were safe and able to look out for themselves.

One day, when the snow had nearly disappeared from the higher valleys and one could walk on dry grass again, Ted sought out White Calf and told him of his desire to return to Spitzee as soon as he possibly could. White Calf knew how the young man felt, and said nothing to discourage him.

Together they walked through the forest, pausing now and then to look at the queer 'stumps' of old bear tracks that stuck high above the ground like misshapen stones. When in the early spring the bear came from his winter den, his great feet compressed the snow beneath them and packed it hard, so that when the warm days came and the softer snow melted, it left the hard-packed tracks standing up for many days more, and in some places the woods were filled with the strange grey mounds.

Ted wanted White Calf to go back to Spitzee with him, but the Indian refused.

"My place is with my family and my people, Sukanabi," he said quietly.

"Then, if you will not come back with me, will you go on a last hunt with me into the mountains?"

"I would be more than pleased to hunt in the mountains with you," replied White Calf; and so it was agreed.

Two days later the young men set out toward the west, and in three hours were climbing over the rocks beside a narrow creek. As they went higher and higher up the stream, the cliffs grew taller on both sides, and soon shut out the sun, leaving only a long slash of blue sky above them. When they came to the pass through the mountains, they sat and rested for a while; then Ted felt a sudden impulse to climb the hill behind them, and White Calf smiled agreement. They laboured up the rocky slope until suddenly there was no more hill to climb and they stood at the top.

From this point Ted could look out over the valleys and lower hills, right down to the camp, right out to the horizon. They sat without moving or speaking, and a strange feeling closed around Ted. He said nothing to his friend, and for some time they just sat there. The sun was bright above them, and only a hundred feet away, against the rock of the mountain, lay the great dirty-white patch of snow that fed the stream they had followed. Grass showed green in places, and already the hardy, tiny white mountain flowers were blossoming.

"White Calf," said Ted hesitantly, "I—I don't really care whether or not we do any hunting. I just wanted to—well—oh, I don't know."

"You only wanted to get away and be alone with your thoughts," suggested White Calf.

"Why—yes, I guess that's about it. Do you feel that way too?"

"When one of my people does not know what to do, or when he is ready to go from childhood into manhood, he goes away by himself, to a lonely place, like the top of a high mountain or a deep canyon, where there is no one but him and God. And there he talks with God, and sometimes God makes him see wonderful things, so that the man may go back to his family and tell what he has seen." Here the Indian paused and stared at the ground, as though arranging his thoughts.

"My ancestors believed," he went on, "that a man's whole life could be told from these visions. They believed that the Great Spirit, whom you call God and we call Napeo, would appear to them if they prayed hard, and would show them how to live the life he had planned for them. My family still believe in this, and our young men all make their vows and keep their vigil alone for a fortnight.

"I myself have spent such a vigil; and I think there is great power in such solitude. When a man has a mind full of fear and doubt, and when his burden becomes too great to carry, sometimes camping on top of a mountain can teach him to think and see things more clearly than if he tried to think while others were near. It is good to spend some time with one's self."

"You are very wise, White Calf. Thank you for teaching me this lesson. May we stay for a little while?" Ted spoke very quietly, for suddenly the whole countryside within his view seemed peaceful and holy. For the first time in his life the white boy had been given an insight into the soul of an Indian, and he realized that he had seen something that few white men would ever see. He bowed his head and thought of all the trials and dangers that an Indian had to face throughout his life; and he knew that here, on a hill that brushed the sky, was the place where the savage came to worship, to ask his Great Spirit for strength, to forge the courage and faith that were his only weapons against a lifetime of hardship.

Chapter Twenty-three

WHEN Ted finally said good-bye to the Stonies, he headed eastward toward the plains. He carried his long rifle across his arm in the manner of the plainsman, and at his side swung his old hunting pouch, stuffed with dried meat, pemmican and other supplies to last him his journey. His moccasins were of new yellow elk hide, tough and well made, while on his back was a robe of rabbit and fox pelts. The morning was warm and bright, and little snow could be seen except in the deepest shade. Ted's heart was light, and once again he thought of the happy song the *voyageurs* sang on the river:

> *En roulant ma boule, roulant,*
> *En roulant ma boule ...*

His voice had a strange ring as he walked easily along the hillsides, but he sang all the louder, not caring that all the creatures in the forest would hear him and run far away. The only time he stopped singing was when he climbed a hill, but after standing on the crest for a moment to regain his breath, he burst out again and sang all the way down. Finally he ran out of songs to sing, and grew tired of singing the old ones over and over again. For several miles he walked in silence, listening to the sounds of life around him. From time to time he sat on a rock or stump, not to rest, but to look and listen.

From one such seat he could see far down into the valley he was following, and in the distance the thin thread of waterfall flashed in the sunlight. And as he watched, a movement caught his eye. A mile or so down the valley a man was walking. From the clothing Ted could tell that it was a white man. For a moment he had the desire to cry out to the fellow, and run down to him as fast as he could. But instantly he checked the impulse, for white men in the hills might, or might not, be friends.

Then a second man joined the first, and the two seemed to be bent on some kind of errand. Ted squinted against the sun, trying to make out what was going on, but it was too far down the slope to the valley floor, even for his keen eyes. The only thing to do was get closer. He slipped from his seat on the hillside and crept slowly down the hill until he was on a level with the men, and hidden behind some trees.

With as much caution as he felt necessary he moved close to the place where the men had been. As he crouched in the scrub pine Ted listened, and in a moment heard the voices. He moved closer, and listened harder. Now the voices were within a hundred yards, and the hidden lad could make out some of what was being said, but the men were moving away from him and he followed.

"Another week like this an' we'll be cleaned out," came a dry voice.

"Yeah, reckon we'll have to make another trip sooner'n we expected. Good thing we got here early, though. Them other fellers are gonna try mighty hard to cut in on our territory."

"Don't you worry none about them other fellers. We got all the customers we need. Only thing is, wish we didn't have to hide the stuff here in the hills. Makes it so far to haul out."

The men walked on a little farther, with Ted following as close as he dared. He did not know what they were talking about, but he knew it must be some kind of trade goods, for the next words told him they were doing business with Indians farther to the south. And that mention of 'other fellows'! He wondered what it meant. Well, the only way to find out was to follow and see what was going on. If these men were honest traders, he would be pleased to join them and travel a way with them. Before he could think of anything else, the men turned off the trail and Ted saw that they had gone to a small cabin built close under the cliffs.

The shack was built roughly of stones and roofed over with logs and earth, and the holes that gaped between the stones showed him that it was not built for winter shelter. Beside the hut stood a large wagon. The men were just at the cabin door when Ted stopped at the edge of the clearing. They went inside, and the boy crouched down again, to wait for whatever might happen further. In a few minutes the men came out again, and this time they went directly to the wagon. A canvas sheet covered the back of the wagon, and when it was thrown aside, Ted could see a number of small round casks inside. He gasped and ducked low into the brush. He knew what the men were up to. The wagon was loaded with whiskey kegs.

Through his mind flashed the sight of his father's post, flaming in the night, and the sounds of drunken natives rang out again in his ears as he pictured them dancing madly around the house, screaming in their frenzied demands for more whiskey. He remembered the fort at the Medicine Trees, and how the whiskey peddlers had been attacked again and again, and finally driven out and their fort burned. And Ted could never forget the scores of Indian skeletons he had seen, and the burial rings and cairns on the hillsides.

This was evidently a large cache of the evil stuff, and the wagon was loaded for another trading venture somewhere on the prairies. Ted could stand the sight no longer, and almost without his realizing it, his rifle came up and levelled at the men. The first inkling they had that they were being watched was when one of the kegs being carried suddenly jumped, and spouted a leak. The explosion that followed sent them diving for cover behind the wagon, around which they cautiously poked their pistols.

Ted was a little dazed by what he had done. In his anger he had been very foolish, and for the moment he did not know what to do. Before he could decide, the whiskey peddlers made up his mind for him. The little glade rang with shots and curses as they fired rapidly at Ted's hiding place. With lead and chips flying on all sides, he turned and beat a hasty retreat into the trees. After a while the shots ceased, and Ted knew they were reloading. He took advantage of this chance to put as much distance as possible between himself and them.

When he felt that it was safe to stop, he sat on the grass and reloaded his rifle, thinking all the while about what he should do. The Stonies would be very angry to learn about this. The best thing to do was to go as fast as possible to White Calf's band and tell them all about it. Perhaps they might stage a raid and drive out the traders. Accordingly he set off up the valley again, retracing his steps. The sun went down long before he reached the top of the hill, and he slept that night under a pine tree.

Before the day broke he was again on the trail. He travelled fast now, stopping seldom, and pushing on so quickly that before dark he came to the Stony camp. Rather, he came to where the Stonies *had* camped. The valley was deserted; they had moved on. It was too late that night to follow farther, so Ted made himself comfortable on the abandoned pine boughs and ate some of his dried meat.

On the next morning he made a circle of the camp, looking for signs to show which way the Indians had gone. If they had owned horses it would have been much easier, but when Indians moved in moccasins across fresh grass and pine needles, it was hard to trace them. At last he picked up the trail, for in some places the grass had been crushed against stones, and rocks had been rolled a little out of place.

The track led into the same coulée where he and White Calf had gone on the day before Ted left camp. Up the same narrow way it led, until he could pick out the very hilltop where they had sat together. But before he came to the slope, the trail turned off and climbed up another gulley, and Ted realized that he was coming to another pass into the mountains. He followed the creek, which now flowed westward, down between the ranges.

The valley or canyon became deeper as he walked, and the cliffs squeezed him in until he sometimes walked in the water, sometimes with one foot on the slope of each bank. This defile soon broadened out into a canyon with a floor about twelve feet wide, and above him the cliffs closed together again, shutting out most of the daylight. A short distance ahead he caught sight of trees, and beyond, the widening of a valley.

Suddenly he was startled by the hail of the lookout, and a moment later the camp came into view. It was located in a large grove of what the white men called "lodgepole pine", for these trees were very long and slender, with no branches for many feet up the trunks, and only a tiny ball of foliage at the top. They were highly valued for the erection of tepees.

As White Calf came to meet him, Ted called out urgently: "White Calf! Whiskey traders are back. They're bringing it in by the wagon-load now."

"That is very bad news, Sukanabi," said the Indian in a grave voice. "Let us go to my father and you will tell him."

Together they strode to a tepee that stood close under a group of dark firs. Ted waited outside while White Calf ducked through the doorway. The rumble of voices came through, and in a few moments White Calf put his head out and said to Ted:

"My father says you must come into his lodge and speak with him about this thing."

Ted bent and entered the tepee. Many Horses spoke softly, for all the tribe were fond of this white youth who had shared their hardships with them during the past winter.

"Sukanabi, my son tells me that you have seen the evil white men who enslave our people with fire water. I would hear the tale from your tongue. Speak!"

Ted repeated what he knew of the white men he had seen in the foothills. At the end of his story the Indian remained silent for a while. Then:

"Our chief must know of this. We shall go to him at once."

And so saying, the elder Indian rose and went out of the tent, with White Calf and Ted behind. They walked directly to the largest tepee in the camp, and both young men waited while the father went in to greet his chief. When Ted was told to enter, he did so, to face several of the elders of the tribe, those who had not died during the winter. They were the counsellors of the band, and had met to discuss the future movements of the camp. When Ted came, they listened to his story. There followed a long period of silence, finally broken by the chief.

With short, determined words he spoke his mind, and with the agreement of his council it was decided that a party of the younger braves should be sent to destroy the whiskey camp and, if necessary, kill the traders. Ted was appointed guide for the party, and within half an hour all the men in the camp were gathered around a council fire.

Ted had never seen Stonies on the warpath. He knew that they could be merciless and terrible at times, and he remembered the raid on the Blackfoot camp. While he listened, ten young warriors were chosen from the best of the band. All the weapons in the camp were brought forward, and each youth chose the best he could find. They wore what they needed for warmth, and carried nothing but their weapons and a small amount of dried meat, for this was to be a fast trip. Broken Shield, the chief, spoke to the gathered men.

"These are evil white men. They are our enemies. We must send our warriors against them to drive them out of our country. They must not remain alive in our land. It may be death to attack them, for they have many guns and much powder. But we of the Stony nation must be as brave as our ancestors who captured this land from our other enemies. We must ask Napeo, the Great Spirit, to send our men strength to do this deed."

Then the Indians were on their feet, forming a circle around the fire, and the white youth watched the first war dance he had ever seen. As the minutes passed the dancers leaped and whooped madly, working themselves into a frenzy, convincing themselves that they were not afraid of this mission. Ted stood watching until with a wild yell the young men broke from the howling ring and ran off up the valley. The raid had started. Ted followed the ten natives, knowing they would soon tire of running and he could catch them in a mile or two.

Even when they did slow their pace, they moved rapidly up the narrow trail, for they had been well chosen. They were the youngest and best of the tribe, and were dedicated to their duty, even though it meant death for some or all. They walked and trotted all that day, moving on soft moccasins up the canyon and out into the green of the foothills.

Chapter Twenty-four

THE trail was rocky but they made good time, although the hills were steep and there was much water in the streams they crossed. Suddenly Ted recognized the landmark and struck off on the dim trail heading straight south. The Indians followed soundlessly, and no word passed between them. For another hour they walked and ran, until Ted was sure they were getting very close to the valley.

He held up a hand in silent caution, and the file of warriors slowed to a walk. Ted headed up the hill, and from the crest he could see the valley. The far end, where the cabin stood, was out of sight around a slight bend, but even from this high point they could see the marks of wagon tracks. They shifted weapons from hand to hand and followed Ted as he led them behind an outcrop of stone, through a dense patch of firs, and down into the valley.

On the floor they stayed in the dark of the woods, moving slowly and furtively toward the end of the valley. No sound or movement came from the cabin. Even when they rounded the corner and saw it against the far trees, nothing moved to alert them. They reached the building, and discovered why. The cabin was empty. The shelves were bare of the kegs they had held.

Men, whiskey, wagon and team were gone. The pursuers would have to trail and try to intercept the party without being seen. All the whites had rifles and pistols, while Ted was the only one of the raiders with a firearm. It would not stand up too well against the repeating rifles of the traders unless they could be taken by surprise. Ted did not want to hurt or kill the men, but if they could be overtaken and surprised in camp, in the dark, perhaps the firearms could be captured, the wagon and contents destroyed, and the horses taken back to the Stony camp. It was a worthwhile attempt.

Almost before they had started looking they found the wheel tracks, for the men had made no attempt to hide their trail. It led into another valley, heading eastward toward the plains. The land was low and flat between the hills and the wagon tires had cut deeply into the sod, making the trail easy to follow. They kept moving until dark, and even then did not stop, for they looked for the bright spark of fire in the distance. Dense trees hid all sight of such a light, but White Calf and Ted climbed the hill and, sure enough, far up the valley they spotted the flicker of the campfire.

Almost running, the war party moved in on the unsuspecting traders. From a hundred yards away the fire looked like a great torch in the blackness of the night. The whites were fond of big fires. They cared little that it might attract attention from miles around. They had camped close beside a little creek and the wagon stood on the bank. The Indians spread out all around the camp, each man knowing exactly what he was to do, each young brave eager for his first great adventure. They ringed the firelight, and as they moved in cautiously they saw the white men preparing their bedrolls. There were five men, and Ted recognized the two he had seen at the shack. The others were strangers, and he could not see their faces clearly in the dancing light. The raiders crept closer, moving almost by silent command. The white men settled down for the night, crawling into their blankets laid in a circle around the fire. For a quarter of an hour all was silent save for the snorting of the horses. Then Ted stepped out into the clearing, the signal for attack.

With screams of savage hate the young Indians leaped from their hiding places, swinging clubs and spears as they went. In an instant three of the traders were on their feet, and the natives rushed toward them. Then the fourth trader sat up in his blankets. The Indians caught sight of him, and stopped in their tracks. A dead silence fell upon the whole camp. It lasted only until one of the Stonies could catch his breath.

"Black white man!" he screamed in terror. "Black bad spirit!" And he turned and fled. He was not alone, for upon his first move the others followed his lead, and left the dazed Negro staring after them, white eyes rolling wide in fear. For an instant Ted was left standing alone against the traders, who began to realize what was happening. Then he chose the wise course, and leaped after his native friends.

It was long past midday before all the Indians were together again. Ted looked at them in the bright sunlight. Their paint was smeared and dirty. They hardly dared look him in the face, but it was White Calf who helped explain things.

"This is no demon, this black white man!" he told them gently. "Sukanabi, tell them what we learned in the white man's school." Ted laughed. He thought of the terror on the faces of his friends, and the look of sheer horror in the white eyes of the Negro. The Indians looked at him in wonder. Here was a leader who did not grow angry when his warriors turned into old women. He did not berate them or beat them with his spear. He only spoke to them.

"It is true, my brothers. This is no evil spirit. In the country far to the south there are many such as he. He is only a man such as the others, but his skin is black instead of white, or red, or brown. He was as frightened of you as you were of him." The Indians seemed to take a little heart at this, but still they sulked fearfully, looking to the woods and shadows as if they expected to find the Negro there.

"Well now," said Ted, finally, "now that you are no longer afraid of the black white man, we must go back again to these whiskey peddlers, and drive them out of our country as we had planned."

"I do not feel well in my legs. I could not walk that far," complained one young man.

"Nor I," exclaimed another.

"I have lost my medicine!" suddenly came the cry from another, who feverishly searched the long grass as if to find his lost charm. Immediately the rest of the Indians set up a clamour.

"To lose one's medicine is a bad omen," they declared.

"We cannot take such a chance. Perhaps we shall have the bad fortune to lose our own."

"Let us return to our village and pray for a vision," suggested another. Ted could see that they would not return to fight the traders, so he did not waste time arguing. White Calf shrugged helplessly and they turned back toward the mountains. Then Ted remembered his mission to Spitzee, and bade good-bye again to his friends.

Ted did not know exactly how far it was to the Spitzee, but he knew that the river lay somewhere to the north, along the first range of mountains. Accordingly he set out along the foothills, and just before dark he came to the river. That night he camped on the bank, and next morning followed down the stream. Another night he spent beside the river, not far above the island of the Medicine Trees. Long before sunrise next morning he was up and on the way, walking slowly so that he could see what was ahead, and before midday was in sight of the new house. His long hail brought a shout from the cabin, and in a moment two figures ran out.

Corteau was the first to recognize the boy, and his yell should have sent the whole Blackfoot Nation on the warpath. James, too, cried loudly across the field when he saw his son sprinting lightly down the path to the clearing. The meeting of father and son brought tears to old Corteau's eyes, for both James and the French-Canadian had believed that Ted had died in the fire. Now they were together again, and ready to start the work of another year.

"Boy, boy! I'm plenty glad for see you, I'm tole you, leetle sparrow!" René thumped Ted on the back, laughing and talking at the same time. James wrung the boy's hand again and again.

"Well, lad, you had us worried this time. We felt sure we had lost you for good."

"No such luck!" grinned Ted, feeling a warm glow of relief. He was going to say more about his stay with the Indians, but suddenly his thoughts turned to the whiskey traders. "Father!" he cried. "I have something important to tell you."

"Important, eh?" James winked at René. "Not getting married, are you, Son?"

"Married?" asked Ted, bewildered at the suggestion. Then he caught the joke. "No. Nothing like that. It's really serious, though. I'm afraid I've got some bad news."

"Well, bad news never gets better for not telling," smiled James, with a tiny wrinkle of worry in his brow. Ted took a breath and explained.

"The whiskey traders are back!" Both men jumped at this statement.

"In Spitzee Anota?"

"No, but very close to it. I ran across a camp of them in the hills, and they're bringing the stuff in by wagon-loads. And last year, remember, I said they were thinking of opening the post at the Trees again. Father, we've got to do something to stop them. They're murdering most of the Indians in the hills, and turning the rest into bloodthirsty drunkards."

James held up a restraining hand to calm his son.

"Steady, lad," he soothed. "It's bad news, to be sure, and something must certainly be done about it. But I have an idea we won't have to."

"What do you mean, Father?" Ted could hardly believe that the elder MacDonnell would refuse to take action against such conditions.

"I mean, perhaps it won't be necessary for *us* to do anything about it," replied James.

"Do you think the Indians will run them out of the territory?" Ted grew excited again. "I tried to lead some of them to do that; but, Father, do you know what? They've got a black man with them. And the minute my Indians saw him, with his white eyes rolling at them, they turned and ran. They think he's some kind of evil spirit. They won't go near that camp again. We can't count on the Stonies this time, and I doubt if there are enough Blackfeet close by to do much good now."

"I didn't mean the Indians would drive them out, Ted." He glanced at Corteau. "There's another outfit that might do the job for us."

"Who is that, Father?" Ted looked from one man to the other, and it was Corteau who answered him.

"You' fadder, he mean dat dere are soldiers come from de East now. Mebbe dey weel feex dose bad man, eh?"

"Right, René. At least we'll hope so," replied James.

"Soldiers!" cried Ted. "Not the soldiers like the ones who drove the Indians up here from the south? I've heard of them. All they want to do is kill the Indians. We'll have more trouble than we have now."

"Wait a minute, Son. Don't get so worked up. I know you are fond of your Indian friends, but you needn't fear these soldiers. They are ours, from Ottawa. And they're coming to make peace in this country, to drive out the bad traders and make the country safe for settlement. We'll hope they learn of your friends with the load of whiskey. They'll do their best to wipe out such lawlessness."

"But, Father, how can they find these fellows? They've got a cabin hidden in the hills, and even I have trouble getting there. Someone will have to show them where it is."

"Dat's right, Jeem. An' ol' Corteau, hees know jus' de feller for be de guide, I'm t'eenk." He winked at Ted, and James nodded his head slowly.

"I guess you're right, René. If we are going to live in this country and hope for law, we had better do our duty to our new protectors. And what better way than to help them, eh, René?"

"Oui, Jeem. Dat is very true. We help dem all dey want, eh?"

"Yes, we must do what we can," cried Ted. "I'll get going right away."

"Wait a minute, young man," his father cautioned. "You've only just got home from a long trip. You can't go out again without some rest and some good food under your belt. We'll leave in the morning."

"We?" repeated Ted.

"We!" said James firmly. "Now that we've got you back again, don't think you're going to run off and leave us to miss all the fun. We'll get in on this party too, eh, René?"

"You bet yo' my life!" René spat on the ground and grinned widely. "We got to take leetle holiday sometime. W'at you say, Ted?"

"I say great!" grinned Ted back at him. "I'll be real glad to have you with me again. What's for supper?"

They went inside the house, and during their meal James explained more about the soldiers who were coming.

"I heard about them in Edmonton, but we thought it was just a rumour. Then when René went back last fall they were already there. Seems like they're not exactly soldiers, though. They call them police, René says. Seems like some kind of Government fellow went all through these parts a few years back and saw what was going on. His report really set the Government back on its heels, I guess, for they up and voted to set up a police force to run the illegal traders out of Canada and to stop all the whiskey trade and the killing and raiding that's been going on for the last while.

"Looks like things are going to be real quiet pretty soon. We'll be able to finish the farm buildings and maybe bring your mother down here next year. How would that suit you, Son?"

"I think it is the most wonderful thing I ever heard of. I hope those fellows know what they are getting into, though. It's pretty rough down south, especially around Whoop Up."

"You don't have to worry about Whoop Up any more," MacDonnell said. "Part of the force arrived there at the same time the others got to Edmonton. All they found at Whoop Up was one man. Name of Aken, or something."

"Aker," Ted corrected him. "I met him there. Where were all the others?"

"Don't know!" shrugged James. "They just faded out of sight, I guess, when they heard the police were coming. Must have thrown quite a scare into them. I don't know about our Indians, though. They hate the sight of a soldier. They're afraid that these men will be the same as the others, and drive them out of their lands and homes. The police claim they are here to fight for the red man as well as the whites, though, and we'll have to try to make the natives trust them. That will be our part of the job."

"Where are these police camped now?" asked Ted.

"Oh, they built a strong fort beside Whoop Up. I guess they will build forts at each end of the country and patrol

the territory in between. Well boys, what say we turn in?"
And so saying, they rolled into their blankets and fell
asleep.

Next morning they left the cabin early. Ted was thrilled
to be riding a horse again, for he had had enough of walking. He slung his rifle across the pony's back and rode
happily up the river bank behind the others. They
travelled steadily for half a day, until Ted called a halt.

"What do you think is the best plan?" he asked. "We
can go up to the hideout and see what is going on, and one
of us can ride out to Whoop Up, or the new post, and get
the police. The other two can follow the whiskey traders
so they don't get away."

"Sounds like a good idea, Ted," replied MacDonnell.

"Oui, my fren'. Dat sound pretty good to me, yo' bet,"
said René.

So they travelled on toward the south. Only a few days
before, Ted had gone this way for the same purpose, and
now he was returning to finish the mission he had set himself. They moved swiftly over the uneven land, following
the hillsides as much as possible so as to stay down and out
of sight of any possible lookout. Ted pulled to a halt just
below the last hill, and they dismounted to creep forward
on foot.

Before them the long valley lay silent in the midday
sun. Nothing moved at the far end where the hut stood.
Ted crept ahead, and in a moment he motioned the others
to follow. He showed them a dense growth of trees all along
one side of the valley, and they led their horses through
these woods, moving closer to the cabin.

When they came through the trees, Ted could see that
the hut had been partly weatherproofed, as though the

men had intended to stay for a while. The wagon stood near one side, the horses in the corral at one end. Smoke poured from the chimney and in a moment a man came out. It was the Negro. He went into the hut again, and from the sounds they guessed that he was preparing a meal. Evidently he was waiting for someone, and in a few minutes the watchers heard the sound of hooves on the valley floor.

The riders galloped up to the cabin and climbed wearily from their mounts. They were the same two men Ted had first seen. They turned their horses into the corral with the rest, then they walked slowly toward the door. Ted could hear them talking.

"Wonder if Bond got here yet. Must have. Fire's lit."

"Reckon so. He's shore handy with a skillet. Makes a better cook than a guide, I'm thinkin'."

"Yeah, but we'd have had more trouble with the savages if he warn't here to talk with 'em. Shore glad we brung him along."

"Yeah. Wish Johnson would get back, though. We got to get that load out of here tomorrow or it'll be risky with them redcoats hangin' around the border."

"Them blasted Mounties will make a lot of trouble. But I reckon we'll make out all right. They ain't got no idea we're hid out here." They passed into the hut and the watchers could hear no more.

"Tomorrow!" muttered James. "They're taking it out tomorrow. We've got to get the police down here as soon as possible. Ted, lad, do you think you can do that stunt of yours again? Like you did to the Indians the first year we came?"

"You mean crawl in on them without being seen?"

asked Ted. His father nodded. "I think so. They don't have a sentry out. Why?"

"Well, I'll ride for the police right now, and you try to stall them off somehow, so they can't take that wagon to-morrow. Do anything you can to stop them long enough for me to get to the post. René, you stay and help Ted. I'll be off now." And he led his pony away around the hill, out of sight. Ted and René watched him go; then they talked quietly of what they should do.

"Maybe if I crawled in and loosened a wheel——"

"De wheel, she's plenty easy for put on again. An' be-sides, dey would know eet was done by a man. Den dey would look for us."

"Yes, I guess that's right. What do you think?"

"I'm t'eenk de bes' way is turn de horses loose. But we mus' make heem look like accident."

"Yes, we don't want them getting on to us before the police are here. We'll have to figure some way to let one or all of them out of the corral as though they did it them-selves. Or maybe we could pretend a bear frightened them, or something."

"I tell you w'at we do. We let de top rail down on one place, like it fall, and it be low so de horse dey can step over. Den we scare dem and dey stampede an' jump de fence an' we hide an' watch dem catch de horse, eh?"

"That's the idea, René. And I've got just the system to make them run, too. Come on, let's get back behind the corral and wait for dark."

They moved quietly through the shadows until they were hidden around a corner of the hill. As the sun moved farther west the day grew darker, until soon the valley was in deep afternoon shadow. As the sun set, the warmth of the day quickly gave place to cooler night air, and in a little while it was dark enough for their purpose. They rested a while longer, waiting until the men would be asleep, and then Ted laid off his heavier clothing, which might make a rustle in the silence, and began his trip to the corral gate.

This work was nothing new to the lad. He had crept unnoticed into the middle of an Indian camp and stolen their horses, and he had stalked the Indians in their own haunts, and hunted the animals of the forest many times. Under cover of darkness it was a simple thing to creep close to the silent hut, where it joined the rude corral. The enclosure was made of logs, perhaps five feet high, with three long poles thrust through the end post to fit into holes in the walls of the hut. These three poles formed the gate by letting down the bars. Ted reached the corner post and very carefully eased to a standing position so that he could touch the top log. The horses sensed him then, and began to stamp and snuffle in alarm. He froze in his position until they got wind of him and quieted, for they were used to man-smell.

While he waited for them to become more at ease, he was able to count them, and was quite surprised to note how many there were. Then he put his hands under the topmost log and began to draw it from the resting place in the wall. As the log moved, it scraped across stone, making a shrill squeak. Instantly Ted released his hold and dropped beside the gatepost, in deeper shadow. He waited.

No sound of alarm came from the cabin, so he stood up again and this time was careful to lift the log a little as he slid one end free. Holding the loose end against him, he gently and slowly lowered it to the ground on the outside of the fence, so that it would look as though the horses had pushed it out of place. The dropped log made a low place in the fence that was not more than three feet high, plenty low enough for a horse to step over. Then he cautiously sank back into the shadows and returned to his place beside Corteau.

"Dat ees pretty good job, Ted. Now all we got to do ees make dem run, eh?"

"Yes. But it will not be too hard. Let's get around to the back side of the corral so they'll run straight at the gate." The two slunk along the edge of the trees until they were directly opposite the gate.

"Well, I'm guess eet ees time to start de fun," observed René.

"I have a trick I learned from the Indians," whispered Ted. He took a bundle from under his arm and unrolled it. It was his blanket, and he laid it on the ground, smoothing it so that it lay flat on the grass. "When I was with the Indians I saw them use blankets to stampede buffalo over a cliff. I guess the same idea will work for horses, even though we can't make a noise by snapping the blanket. The movement alone should scare them."

"By gar, dat's right. I'm see dem do dat myself. Good boy, Ted. Geeve her de try."

Ted stepped to one edge of the blanket and grasped two corners, then raised them and gave the blanket a long, smooth flip. It rose like a dark ghost in the starlight, making a heavy whoosh as it flapped. Instantly the corral burst into activity, for the horses were already spooky from Ted's prowling. It took only the sight of the unknown dark thing moving near them to send them into a terrified fury. With

squeals like angry bears they charged away from the unknown danger, and piled up against the gate.

Then the watchers saw that their plan was going to work
even better than they had hoped. The press of horseflesh
against the flimsy poles was too much, and the whole side
of the enclosure began to sway. As hundreds of pounds of
horse strained against it, the fence gave way, falling outward with a great clatter. The noise of the breaking fence
added to the fright of the poor beasts and they fell in a
struggling heap. As soon as they realized that they were
free, they jumped to their feet and thundered up the valley,
running wildly in all directions, until they reached open
ground and formed behind the herd leader to vanish into
the darkness.

Ted and René moved swiftly back into the underbrush,
for now the sounds of curses and shouts rose from the
house. In a moment the door slammed open and men
tumbled out, half dressed, grasping weapons and stumbling to the corral. By the time they reached it, Ted and
Corteau were far out of sight over the hill, and the horses
were but a cloud of dust that was hidden by the shadows of
night.

Ted did not know what happened back at the cabin, but
no shots were fired, and even though he listened for a long
time, no sound of footsteps told of any pursuit. They had
done the trick and got away with it.

It was late the next afternoon before the tired traders
caught up with their horses and turned them back into the
repaired corral. And by that time it was much too late to
start for the plains. Ted and Corteau grinned silently at
each other, waiting for darkness to fall so that they could
repeat the performance.

But Ted did not get a chance to repeat it. That night the traders put a guard at the corral, to ward off marauding "bears and cougars", and Ted had to spend his time watching, trying to find some way to hold the wagon for another day, to give his father time to reach the police post and return with the men.

Very early that morning the traders began to pack up. Ted and Corteau watched from a safe distance.

"I reckon the police will need to send a whole army to take these fellows," said Ted. "The traders have a whole wagon-load of guns, too, I think, and lots of ammunition. It will take a real fight to stop them, unless we can catch them asleep."

"By gar, I'm bet nobody gone catch dese fellow asleep no more," mourned Corteau. "Dey ain't gone take no chances lose all dose horse dey got, I'm bet yo'." When daylight came the traders set out down the valley toward the plains, and the two shadows followed them, keeping well out of sight. As soon as they saw the valley the wagon would have to go through, they formed a plan, and raced over a hill that hid them from the traders. They sped along as quietly and as quickly as they were able, hoping to head the wagon off at some narrow place on the trail.

They came to a place where the wagon would pass through a narrow space between high banks, and there leaped from their mounts. But when they looked down upon the trail, they were dismayed to see the wagon rolling through the place where they had planned their trap. They were too late.

"René, what'll we do? They're getting away!"

"Nom de nom! We can do not'eeng now. Not'eeng but watch dem go away."

But even as he spoke, a movement on the far hillside drew their attention. A rider appeared, almost as from thin air. He rode directly upon the wagon and the traders stared at him in amazement, so surprised that they did not see the others who rode up from all sides, the scarlet of their tunics like drops of blood against the green of the fir trees. In an instant the traders were surrounded, and covered by menacing rifles.

The driver of the team gave his horses a crack with the whip to spur them on and try to break away from the attackers, but a strong hand grasped the reins of the lead horse and drew the team around in a circle on itself. The wagon was stopped and the traders could only raise their hands. One of their captors, evidently the leader, called out in a loud, clear voice:

"In the name of the Queen, you are under arrest!"

One of the policemen rode close to the wagon and tore the tarpaulin from it. There lay a pile of rifles and pistols, and a large bale of furs that looked like buffalo robes. Kegs filled the rest of the wagon. The policeman replaced the cover, and the leader signalled the traders to start. The red-coated riders formed a solid line on each side of the cowed whiskey peddlers, while two other policemen dropped behind to herd the horses. In a little while the cavalcade was lost to sight around a bend in the trail.

"Sacré nom de petit cochon bleu!" gasped Corteau.

Then another rider appeared from the opposite side of the valley and descended to the trail. It was James. Ted yelled at him, and with Corteau rode down to meet him. The three men sat looking down the valley to where a little cloud slowly settled from the passing of many hooves.

"Quick trip, Father. You got here just in time."

"I didn't get to the post," said James. "I met the police just a few miles away, and they were already waiting for the traders."

"You mean they knew all about it?"

"That's right. Seems as though a Blackfoot runner told them, and it is their first arrest in the territory. And just think, Ted, what effect it will have on the Indians. The soldiers they feared have taken their first prisoners—all white men."

" 'In the name of the Queen!' " breathed Ted. "Then surely this means that law has really come to Assiniboia."

"I'm t'eenk I'm goin' to like dose Mounted Policemen, me," said Corteau. "An' I'm t'eenk I'm goin' to be good fellow from now on, I'm bet yo'."

"Aye, the law has come, lads. And it's time we were heading back to Spitzee. We've a lot of work to do this summer before we go to fetch the lady."

And the three of them rode back up the trail, side by side; and the valley had never seemed so peaceful and happy. The Queen's law had indeed come to the West.

THE END